SEA OF SINNERS

A DARK WHY CHOOSE ROMANCE

BLOOD & SAND SERIES
BOOK 1

HEIDI STARK

Sea of Sinners
Heidi Stark

This is a work of fiction. Any resemblance to real people, living or dead,
organizations, places, events or locals, are entirely coincidental. Although if you
do know four guys like the Brixton men, please send them my way.

Book #1: Blood & Sand Series
Copyright © 2023 Heidi Stark. All rights reserved.

No portion of this book may be reproduced in any form or used in any matter
without written permission from the author, with the exception of brief
quotations in a book review.

IMPORTANT NOTE

Sea of Sinners features triggering situations and mentions including graphic descriptions of violence and sex.

Adoption
Alcoholism
Attempted murder
BDSM
Blackmail
Bullying
Captivity and confinement
Child abuse (mention)
Coercive control
Criminal activity
Daddy/praise kink
Drink spiking
Drugging
Dubcon
Emotional abuse
Gore
Grievous bodily harm
Intrusive thoughts

Kidnapping

Mental health issues

Murder

Organized crime

Psychological abuse

PTSD

Sexual assault (mention of past incidents)

Sexually explicit scenes

Squirting

Stalking

Threats of violence

Torture

Toxic relationships

Trauma

*To the ones who knew one man would never be enough, because you
were never meant to be handled gently.*
You were meant to be taken.
Claimed.
*Surrounded by men who don't soften their edges just to make you
comfortable.*
The kind who see your black heart and want all of you anyway.
The kind who don't ask if you're theirs — they decide.
*The kind who would burn the world for you
and expect you to stand in the flames with them.*
To the ones who wouldn't run.
You were never meant to.

PROLOGUE

She doesn't know it yet… but she's already ours.

We saw her before she ever saw us.

Watched her laugh like she didn't know what kind of place this was. Like this island wasn't built on blood and secrets and men who take what they want.

Angel Benson walks through our world like she's untouchable.

Like nobody has marked her.

Like nobody has claimed her.

That's going to be a problem.

Because we don't share.

We take.

And once we decide something is ours…*we don't let it go.*

CHAPTER 1

ANGEL

The front door jingles as someone enters the salon, and for a moment I take my eyes off my client and glance over to see who it is. It's a guy I haven't seen before, but he strolls in with confidence, as if he's been here many times.

And he is *hot*. Not just kind of good-looking. He's scalding, a clear twelve on a ten-point scale.

Closing the door behind him, his eyes skim the salon and, seeming to pass his invisible standards, he nods almost imperceptibly before making his way further inside.

I wonder what most people's first impressions are when they enter this place. It has everything it needs to give clients what they're looking for, but it's pretty bare bones.

It's a small space, big enough for one hairstylist, two at max, and every surface is cluttered with hair products and equipment and cleaning supplies.

The furniture is secondhand, every table and chair slightly nicked or peeling or getting threadbare if you take a closer look, but people come here for a great haircut, not for a comfortable place to hang out.

And while the salon may not be the height of interior design, I pride myself on making sure everything is clean and sterilized and follows proper health and safety guidelines.

Jars of blue barbicide solution line the walls, reminiscent of the specimen containers you see in biology classrooms where preserved organisms sit suspended in formalin. But in this case, they're filled with combs and scissors and other items that are better off cleansed of human grossness.

The first thing I notice about the hot stranger is his dark hair, longer at the top and swept away from his face, and shorter on the sides and back. Hair that requires taking a fair bit of maintenance, not just a regular short style like most guys want when they come in. He takes care of his hair, and it's clearly important to him. I'm a hairstylist and I notice these things.

His eyes are a striking gray-green, like olive and fog swirled together, and they twinkle as he looks around the salon, his gaze eventually settling on me. Combined with his sexy lopsided smirk, it's almost as if he's in on a joke that nobody else is. He exudes confidence and comfort in his own skin.

He's taller than average, maybe around six-two, and he wears a fitted T-shirt that shows off his well-developed pecs and shoulders. Tattoos cover his muscular arms, which I find sexy as hell. And despite the island heat, he wears dark blue jeans and leather shoes. Not many guys dress this well around here, with everything fitted to his body like it was made for him.

The client I'm working on looks up as well, and her eyebrows involuntarily raise ever so slightly in a sign she thinks he's hot, too. She grins at me in the mirror, and I wink back at her.

I smile and nod in his direction, and call out, "Welcome! I'll be right with you!"

"Good with a pair of scissors, are you?" His eyes roam my body and settle on the shears I'm holding in my left hand.

It's like he doesn't even care I'm working on someone else. Like he expects to have my undivided attention the moment he enters the store.

The way he looks, he probably doesn't have to work for female attention, and he's probably used to getting what he wants when he wants it. Jerk.

"I might be a little while. We still have a bit to do here before we finish up," I say, gesturing toward my client. "Feel free to look at the products on display in the meantime, or you're welcome to take a seat."

I point my shears at the display case beside the cash register to the left of where he's standing, as well as the slightly threadbare couch off to the right side of the front entrance.

I'm not apologetic about making him wait. Whoever he is, I know he doesn't have an appointment, because this is my last booking for the day. I do accept walk-ins, though, and I'd be happy to take a look at his hair once I'm done with my current client.

We don't get a ton of foot traffic here. The salon is located on the second story of a strip mall in a suburb tucked away behind the highway, about a mile from the beach. So if people end up here, it's generally because they've found the salon online or through word of mouth.

I hardly doubt this guy just happened to be strolling through the neighborhood, judging from the way he looks. Someone must have referred him here, although I don't see him being BFFs with any of my regular clients, or he's done his own research. He definitely looks more like a city guy, from a proper bigger city on the mainland rather than the small and low-key one we have here. But he also bears the signature tan of someone who lives here and spends a lot of time in the ocean.

I wonder if he surfs. From the way his muscles ripple under his T-shirt when he moves, it wouldn't surprise me.

He glances over at the glass shelving stacked with gels and waxes, but his gaze quickly returns to me.

"No rush," he says, continuing to survey me. "I'll just watch you work."

As his eyes linger on my ass, a strange look passes over his face, almost like a half-grimace, half-smile, and he suddenly plunks himself down into the couch in the waiting area. A weird, jerky movement that seems to come from out of nowhere, a contrast from the confidence and poise he's exhibited so far.

Unlike most of my other customers, he doesn't pick up a fashion or hairstyle magazine from the pile stacked neatly on the coffee table in front of him, or scroll mindlessly through his phone as he waits. Instead, he continues to watch me, his eyes roaming over my body as I work on my client's hair.

I feel a flush creeping up my chest and neck and onto my face, my body feeling tingly under his gaze. I'm not used to people watching me work.

"It's rude to stare," I say, narrowing my eyes at him. "Can you read a magazine or something?"

"I like what I'm looking at more." His eyes blatantly continue to explore my every angle, and my face grows hotter, the flush intensifying.

"I'm not sure whether that's meant to be flattering or creepy. Can't you see I'm working on my client here?" I roll my eyes at him.

I meet my client's eyes in the mirror as I continue to cut her hair, and she smirks.

"If you'd like me to leave you two alone, I can," she says. I feel myself flush further and my reflection confirms my face has reached tomato-level redness.

"No, of course I don't want you to leave," I quickly reply. "Sorry for this… distraction." My eyes flit to the insanely good-looking man observing me from the couch and then back to my client. "My focus is entirely on you. You're my top priority."

The hot guy smirks and picks up a magazine. He flips the pages and occasionally glances down at a picture or an article, but in the mirror I can see his eyes always quickly return to rest on me. If he wasn't so hot, it might creep me out, but his gaze isn't unwanted.

Because I can be slightly petty, I make sure to give my client the VIP treatment, taking my time on the finishing touches, and giving her a thorough rundown of all the products I used on her today.

I notice that the hot guy wriggles his ankle a little and checks his watch now and then, but he doesn't leave or complain about the wait.

Interesting. I wonder what makes him want to stick around. It's not like this is the only salon in the area.

By the time I'm done with my client, she looks fantastic, and I can tell by her glow and the way she's beaming that the hair revamp has given her a confidence boost.

It's amazing what a few layers, highlights, or even just a conversation with someone who listens for an hour or two, can do to a person's energy. It's the main reason I do this job, my personal avenue for artistic expression.

There have been so many times I've been down on myself and my life circumstances. I know what it feels like to desperately need a little pick-me-up.

Helping other people feel good about themselves is one of the few things within my control. I get to work alone and do things on my terms, with nobody telling me what to do except for the odd bossy client. And I can fire clients if they get to be too much.

Plus, I'm exceptionally skilled with scissors. That helps, too.

CHAPTER 2

ROMAN

Against my better judgement, I'm biting the bullet and trying out a new hair salon today. Despite my apprehension, the moment I enter the space, I'm glad I did. Because even if I end up leaving here with a buzz cut, this hairdresser is hot as hell. At least the view will be enjoyable for an hour or so.

I've been a little stressed the past few weeks, ever since the hairstylist I've trusted for years broke the news that she was moving away. She was one of the few humans I trusted, aside from my business partners, my brotherhood.

It might sound like I'm laying it on a little thick by saying that, but it's the truth. A haircut can make or break someone. She or he who holds the shears and razor blades rules the world, or at least dictates whether I'm going to have a good time for the next few weeks.

My former hairstylist was so worried about telling me she was leaving that she insisted I meet her for coffee away from the salon when she broke the news. I think she was maybe concerned I'd have a temper tantrum and destroy her place. But

I'm not a monster. I just have a vested interest in her work, and I liked the consistency of knowing I could rely on her when I needed her, which was often.

I recall how she trembled as she told me she was heading out of town, and seemed relieved when I didn't try to talk her out of it. She looked surprised as I handed her a generous roll of bills to thank her for holding me down for the past eighteen months or so.

So now I'm a free agent with my hair, which is an uncomfortable place to be.

After extensive online research, I found people had lots of good things to say about this place, so here I am. Nobody mentioned that the hairdresser is a fucking smoke show.

It might sound vain, but I take my face and my hair very seriously. They, and my body which I also keep very much in shape, are what help me get the ladies. And ladies are my primary hobby. Lots of them, all the time. Sometimes several at the same time. I rarely meet one I don't like.

I move in circles where attractive women are plentiful, a mixture of tourists and wealthy folks who live on the island. Owning several upscale clubs and bars gives me access to an endless supply of gorgeous women who take phenomenal care of themselves. They're easy pickings at the venue we own, consistently dressed up and manicured and looking to let loose and have a good time.

Being a club and bar owner is like having a magnet stuck to me that draws women in whenever I'm near. They're attracted to the power and the celebrity of it all, basically dripping and creaming themselves at the chance to be seen on my arm, maybe seeking the heady thrill of being given a complimentary bottle of champagne courtesy of the owner.

It's an all-you-can-eat buffet and I like to feast often.

Having fantastic hair only sweetens the deal. Self-maintenance is worth the investment, and I can afford it, so why not?

As soon as I see the hairstylist in this new salon, I can't keep my eyes off her. I know it's rude to stare, but I'm attracted to beautiful things. And she is really fucking gorgeous.

Her hair is a vibrant purple that contrasts vividly with her creamy complexion. She wears bright red lipstick that showcases her plump lips. She beams a wide, bright megawatt smile at me in a friendly welcome, her teeth straight and white. Long lashes frame her large green eyes, and her high cheekbones are stunning.

As she works on her client's hair, I can see her from the side, as well as her reflection in the mirror. She makes conversation with her client, smiling frequently, and I notice she has a dimple on one of her cheeks. Adorable and sexy.

She's wearing a short green denim shirtdress that hugs her curves and has a slightly military look to it. Her reflection shows a hint of cleavage, and it looks like she maybe has a tattoo chest piece hiding under there that I want to see more of.

She has a nose and lip piercing, as well as countless piercings in her ears, some of them connected by small chains. And while I love a lot of things about women, I'm a particular sucker for tattoos and piercings.

The more I look at her, the more things I notice that I like, and the more she captivates my attention.

Blood rushes to my cock and makes me hard, and my heart beats faster, just at the sight of her. She's having a stronger effect on me than most women, just being in her presence. I wonder if she smells like citrus or vanilla or bergamot or rose. I wonder if her hands are delicate and gentle or strong and purposeful.

Hopefully, she finishes up with this client soon, because I want to be near her, to see her up close, and to learn more about her.

To see why I'm reacting to her in this way. She's sexy, but she's a stranger, and we haven't even spoken yet. I need to know more.

Because as much as I like women, I'm always in control. I'm the one making their pulse race, making them aroused when I choose to. Taking my time to tease, or just grab what I want with no preamble, depending on my mood.

I dictate the pace, what happens, when it happens, and how it happens. Everything that takes place is because I make it so, and I decide how my body responds in every situation.

But one look at this woman and I'm a mess with a throbbing cock, practically salivating on the floor. I can't tear my eyes away from her.

She's a masterpiece. And I want her.

CHAPTER 3

ANGEL

I check my happy client out at the cash register, and she beams as she hands me a generous tip for my work with her today, insisting we get her next appointment locked into the calendar.

As soon as she leaves the salon, I pick up the broom and start sweeping the locks and hair fragments discarded during the haircut into a pile in the middle of the floor. I sweep the pile up with a dustpan and brush, and start to reset my station for the next client.

As I wipe the counter down and hang the hairdryer back up on its hook, I turn to Hot Guy, who's still on the couch observing me while poorly pretending to read a magazine. "So you want your hair cut, or do you just like to stare at strangers while they're working?"

Without being invited, he strolls over to my hairdressing chair and plonks himself down right in front of me while I'm still setting up. "You made me wait long enough. I'm invested now. And it's not my fault you're pretty to look at. Beautiful, even."

Oh, so he's one of those. A charmer. Knows all the smooth

things to say to the ladies. I know his type, and have him pegged a mile away. I bet he gets away with it too, with his egregiously good looks.

I lower the chair by pumping the lever with my foot. He's a lot taller than my last client.

Wrapping a hairdressing cape around him and securing it carefully at the back, I run my hands through his hair to see what I'll be working with. It's soft, and I vaguely recognize the masculine, unique scent of his pomade as cognac and Cuban cigars.

I face him in the mirror and he maintains eye contact while I try to get a sense of what he wants today. "What are you looking for? Sticking with the taper fade with slick back?"

I run my fingers through the lengths of his hair, my nails gently scratching his scalp as I get a feel for its thickness and the direction it grows.

"That feels good," he says. "And is that what it's called? Taper something or other? I just call it my hair." He shrugs and smirks at me in the mirror.

"You keep it in good condition for someone who doesn't know much about it," I smirk back at him. "I think you know more about your hair than you say you do. In fact, based on its current condition I'd venture to say you're quite particular."

"What can I say? I need to make sure I look good for the ladies." He winks at me and grins.

"I'm sure there are a lot of ladies that are interested in your, uh… hair."

My eyes travel over his muscular body and my words trail off as my gaze reaches his crotch. I feel myself blush when I realize he's watching my eyes roam all over him.

He smirks. "Are you interested… what did you say your name was?"

"I didn't. But my name is Angel." I can't resist giving him a hard time. "It's why the salon is called Angel's Hair Salon."

"Clever," he smirks. "And are you an angel, Angel?"

"It's a somewhat ironic name, but I didn't choose it." I shrug. It's a lie. I totally chose it, but he doesn't need to know that. Nobody needs to know that except me. As far as anyone else is concerned, it's been my name since birth.

"Oh, so you think you're a badass?" He raises an eyebrow.

"True badasses never talk about it." I grin.

He smirks again.

I make eye contact with him in the mirror. "So what happened to your last hairdresser? Clearly, you haven't been cutting your own hair at home. Are you new to the island? Or did they fire you because you kept staring at them while they worked on other clients?"

"She moved away, actually," he frowns. "It was traumatic. It happened recently and I'm still grieving a little. I had to scour the internet to find this place. It better live up to all the hype." He says it like he's joking, but I sense some truth to it.

I snort. "It's a salon in a strip mall, not a Beverly Hills boutique. A step up from Great Clips. So maybe set your expectations accordingly."

He smirks. "As long as you don't have a buy nine haircuts get one free coupon, I'm good."

I shake my head to indicate we don't have coupons, and he looks relieved.

"If you fuck up my hair, I'm coming for you, though," he laughs, but it sounds hollow and I shiver at the coldness in his voice.

"Well, that sounds ominous. I'll make sure I do a good job. You just need to be clear about what you want."

He just laughs the hollow laugh again. Weirdo.

"So, help me out here. Do you want the same again, just a little trim?"

"Yeah, this hairstyle seems to be doing the trick. Just a trim will do. We can mix things up a little once we've established a trusting relationship. It's very important to me that I trust my stylist implicitly."

The way he says it sounds like he's picking a neurosurgeon to conduct delicate brain surgery, not just trim the ends of his hair, but whatever.

"We'll do the trust fall exercise at the end of the appointment," I roll my eyes.

He smirks at me in the mirror.

"Alright, let's get you over to the hair washing station." I gesture to the wall of sinks with reclining chairs lined up in front of them. "Second one down."

He gets up and walks to the chair next to the one I pointed to. "I prefer this one. Three's my lucky number."

"Sure," I roll my eyes. "Whatever one you like, snowflake." What a picky asshole. Superstitious too, it seems.

He sits in the recliner, leans back and places his neck in the basin's divot, and I turn on the water.

After testing it on my forearm, I wet his hair, making sure to saturate every lock. "Is the temperature okay?"

"It's a little hot, like you. But I like that," he says, looking up at me, his head still reclined in the sink. He's hot upside-down as well. Jesus.

I massage a blob of shampoo into his scalp, making it lather up into a rich foam, and then rinse it carefully until the water flows clear. I repeat the same with some hydrating conditioner, making sure it coats his hair from the roots to the tips.

"This needs to sit for a few minutes. Would you like a scalp massage while you wait?"

"Is that something you ask all your clients? Or am I getting the VIP treatment?" he smiles.

"I definitely offer it to all my clients. Don't flatter yourself," I say, but I wink at him.

"I thought I was special," he pouts. "But I'd still like to see what you can do with your hands," he grins his upside-down grin and winks back at me.

I massage his scalp, using my fingers and thumbs to knead the top of his head and his neck, and he closes his eyes and leans into my hands. I gently swirl my nails across his scalp, well aware of the tingly sensation this creates, and he sinks his head into my touch.

When I massage just above his ears, making firm circles with two fingers on each side, he lets out a soft groan.

"Fucking hell, Angel," he says. "You're very good at this. Your hands are amazing. I almost fell asleep when you used your nails. I love the way you're scratching my scalp."

"Just doing my job," I shrug, but his words generate a brief flutter in my chest that travels down to my core. There's definitely a little electricity each time my hands touch him.

I carefully rinse the conditioner out of his hair and then towel-dry it, pressing the towel firmly onto his head to gather the excess moisture.

"Right, we're all set." I discard the towel, then guide him back to the hairdressing chair where he sits down again.

I pick up my shears and take another look at his hair, mapping out my approach to his cut.

"So, tell me about yourself, Angel." He eyes me in the mirror. "What do you do other than look drop-dead gorgeous?"

He's back again with the flattery. But this time his words flow a little too easily, and it's clear he's using a line he's spun before. It's something he could say to absolutely any woman to get their heart racing. Gross.

I narrow my eyes at him. "Stop distracting me, or I might accidentally chop off one of your ears."

"I'd be okay with that, as long as you're the one who did the chopping. I don't mind a little knife play." He winks at me.

Jesus, this guy has no boundaries. I've barely known him for thirty minutes and he's whipping out knife play talk. Still, it's kinda hot even if it's a bit unusual for a first-time conversation.

We chit-chat about life on the island. By the sounds of it, he's been here a little under two years.

While the island is relatively small, I'm not surprised we haven't crossed paths, even though we've been here around the same amount of time. Judging from his appearance, he and I run in very different circles. And to be fair, I spend most of my time here at the salon and at my apartment, and occasionally in the ocean when I go surfing. There's limited opportunity to bump into someone new.

As I snip away at his hair, preserving his existing style, my body occasionally presses into his for leverage. Each time it does, his eyes get a little darker, and my body feels a little tingly at the connection.

He mentions owning a couple of clubs in the city and over in the tourist area. I'm past the time in my life when I frequented clubs and bars every weekend, and that phase was long gone by the time I moved here. I only visit the congested tourist area when I have to, or for a special occasion of some sort.

I stick to myself for the most part, and I live in the same suburb as the salon. It's a sleepy area, with pockets of lively cafes and neighborhood restaurants. We have a grocery store and a pharmacy and a hardware store, so there's not really a need to venture much further afield.

Especially when you value alone time as much as I do. And especially when you're trying to keep a low profile, and stay off the radar of someone who might be trying to find out where you are.

The one thing I seem to have in common with Hot Guy, other than a love for good hairstyles, is surfing.

He mentions having grown up on the coastal mainland, and having worked as a surf lifesaver in some fairly treacherous waters when he was a teenager. It sounds like he's enjoying being able to do it every day, living here

I didn't really get into surfing until I moved here. I'd tried it a couple of times when I was growing up, but it was more a case of splashing around with a surfboard for fun and I didn't really know what I was doing.

Here, I've taken a few lessons from locals. It's so casual on the island that people will trade haircuts for surfing lessons, plumbing repairs, home-cooked meals, and pretty much anything else you can think of.

I've made a small group of surfing acquaintances who I head out with a couple of days each week, after I've locked up for the day and headed home from the salon. We like to sit out in the water and watch the sunset while we casually chat about our days, much of the time spent in silence just listening to the gentle voice of the ocean lapping at our boards.

My surfing buddies are very low-key and don't ask a ton of questions. They just want companionship out on the water, which works well for me. I can choose what I want to share, and so I share very little. It's better that way for everyone. And I also enjoy the quiet camaraderie that comes with sitting out in the ocean with a group that will have your back if you need it.

I'm about halfway through Hot Guy's haircut when the door jingles again and another man enters the salon. I've never seen him before, either.

His figure is large and imposing, he's maybe six-foot-four and made of solid muscle, and he breathes heavily underneath his puffy coat.

He has long light-brown hair pulled back in a ponytail, bushy eyebrows and brown eyes that flit around as if he's constantly assessing his environment for threats. I know that look from people who work in security, as well as in restaurant managers. They're always scanning for trouble, having difficulty maintaining focus because they're keeping track of a million little things.

The new arrival has thin lips, and his nose has a prominent bump in it like it's been broken and reset one too many times. An angry red scar protrudes from his jaw and extends down his neck. Whoever he is, this man has been through some things.

He's definitely not one of my usual clients, and I'm not sure why everyone is dressing so warmly today. We're on a tropical island, for goodness' sake.

The man stops for a moment, glancing around the salon.

After establishing the three of us are the only ones in the space, his gaze settles on Hot Guy and his eyes narrow.

"You fucking Brixton scum," he growls, fumbling inside his coat.

"Excuse me? To whom do I owe the pleasure?" Hot Guy cocks his eyebrow.

"You don't need to know who I am," the big guy snarls.

"Well, you clearly know who I am," says Hot Guy. "It's only fair that you introduce yourself as well."

"I'm not here for pleasantries, you piece of shit," he growls. "I'm here to give you and your brothers a message. Except in this case, you'll be the message."

I gasp as he finishes unzipping his coat, pulls a gun from his waistband, and aims it at Hot Guy.

Without flinching, Hot Guy looks over at him through the reflection in the mirror, his back to the man. "Asshole, whoever you are, you're making a big mistake. Put the gun down." His voice is calm and steady.

My heart feels like it's going to beat out of my chest as I glance between the men. I don't dare make a move, and instead, I stand glued to the floor, willing my muscles not to twitch and remind either man I'm here.

"Look, there's no need to be pointing a gun at us, man," says Hot Guy. "You seem like a reasonable guy. Let's just have a conversation. How about you tell me why you're here?"

The Asshole shakes his head. "We don't need to do any talking. My gun will do that just fine."

Hot Guy shrugs. "Sure, that's an option. But how about you tell me more about what's going on, and we can figure things out together? There must be more than one option here. We can work it out. I might be able to help you in some way. Let's just talk about it."

There's a man literally pointing a deadly weapon at us and Hot Guy is unflappable, talking to The Asshole like he's soothing a toddler, trying to reason with him so he'll put the weapon down.

But it doesn't seem to work. The Asshole doesn't answer, and keeps the gun aimed at us. He takes a step closer to Hot Guy. In this cramped space, it's feeling claustrophobic.

"Who sent you?" Hot Guy asks again, his body tensing a little as he sees his efforts to use logic aren't working. The energy is shifting, and Hot Guy's demeanor is quickly transitioning from congenial and helpful to frustrated.

"I work alone." The Asshole's eyes flicker downward. The way he says it doesn't sound convincing. But he juts his chin out as if to double down on his comment.

Hot Guy smirks at the man. "I find that hard to believe."

The Asshole growls and steadies the gun as Hot Guy pivots from trying to reason with him to being straight-up condescending.

"Fuck you, Brixton. You all think you're fucking better than everyone else. Trying to take over the business that we worked so hard to build up over years and years."

"Look, I don't know who you are. But my brothers and I are doing well because we are the best at what we do. We work hard and we get to reap the rewards for our efforts," he shrugs. "I'm not sorry for being strong and powerful, so I will not apologize. I don't care what weapons you have pointed at me."

"You don't just get to come here and take what's ours," The Asshole growls.

"I'm not sure what you're referring to exactly, but if we took something from you, I guess that makes it ours now. That's how things work around here. Again, not sorry."

"You fucking mainland fucks! Coming here and trying to tell us how things are meant to work!" The Asshole raises his voice and clicks off the safety of his gun.

Hot Guy snatches the hairdressing shears from my hand and spins in the chair to face The Asshole. "Come on, Asshole," sighs

Hot Guy. "Put the fucking gun down or things won't end well for you."

The Asshole cocks the hammer of his gun, keeping it trained on Hot Guy.

At that moment, Hot Guy flits to where The Asshole stands, and suddenly my hairdressing shears are embedded deep in the side of The Asshole's neck. His eyes bulge and he groans, his hands flying to the handles of the shears as blood runs from his mouth in a dark red rivulet, trailing down his chin and dripping onto the floor.

"I told you to put the gun down, asshole," hisses Hot Guy. "You really should have listened to me. Your failure to do so is going to be your undoing."

The Asshole lurches forward, arms raised to shoulder height as if he means to attack Hot Guy, and bubbles of blood pop and splutter as they exit his mouth. He makes a terrible gurgling sound that I'm probably never going to be able to fully rinse from my brain.

Hot Guy yanks the knife out of The Asshole's neck, and blood erupts from his carotid in waves of crimson, reflecting the rhythm of his heartbeat.

Jesus. Hot Guy knew exactly where to stab for maximum damage.

Hot Guy circles The Asshole until he's behind him, then grabs him by the ponytail and yanks his head back. The Asshole's eyes grow large and he tries to reach back and free himself of Hot Guy's grasp as Hot Guy raises the shears high in the air and off to one side of The Asshole.

I cry out, "No!" as Hot Guy slices The Asshole's throat from ear to ear. After a moment, while his body catches up to what just happened, blood pools at the gash and then pours forth a violent scarlet waterfall, splattering all over the floor and the Asshole's shoes, some splashing onto Hot Guy's face and clothing.

The Asshole gurgles, "Fuck!" as he falls to the floor, his gun slipping from his grip and clattering to the ground. His body topples and he lands on his front, one of his legs bent and splayed out to the side, an arm stretched upward, prone like a perfect chalk outline at a police crime scene. A pool of crimson forms beneath him.

I stand, hand across my open mouth, as blood continues to drain from his body onto the floor.

I glance around and it's now just me, the Hot Guy, and The Asshole's dead body, squeezed into the cramped salon. The salon is silent except for the tick-tock of a vintage cat clock, its tail and eyes darting from side to side each second. There's no traffic noise, no hustle and bustle of commuters making their way to or from work. Just the tick-tock of the clock and the heavy weight of death hanging in the air.

Hot Guy picks up The Asshole's gun from where he dropped it when he crumpled to the ground, clicks on the safety and slides it into his back pocket.

He then calmly walks over to one of the hair-washing basins on the far wall of the salon and rinses my shears under the running water. He dries them on a towel and casually walks back to where I'm standing.

I'm tempted to reach out and try to grab the shears back from him, but as I try to extend my arm, I realize my hands are shaking violently. Hot Guy just used my beloved work tool to kill someone right in front of me.

He was so calm and controlled, dominating the situation even in the face of death. The way he looked at The Asshole, not flinching while he pointed a deadly weapon at him, was impressive and kinda hot.

But who the fuck is this guy, and why did The Asshole come after him with a gun? I know Hot Guy acted in self-defense, but did the altercation really have to end in murder?

And who's going to clean up the body and the big puddle of blood in the middle of my salon floor?

———

Hot Guy glances around the salon, and then at me, and he sighs.

He walks to the front entrance, locks the door and pulls down the blinds on the door and the window so nobody can see inside.

"What are you doing? The salon is still open."

I stare at him as he tries to take control of what happens in my salon. This is my turf, not his. I don't even know this guy and he's wandering around and trying to dictate my business hours like he owns the place.

He shakes his head. "Not anymore, it isn't."

"What do you mean? I have a business to run. I can't just close the place whenever I feel like it. Clients expect me to be open when I'm meant to be."

"Too bad," he shrugs. "You're coming with me."

"No, I'm not. I have to work."

"You're planning on cutting hair while there's a body and a huge puddle of blood just sitting there?" He gestures at the dead guy and the mess. "And you think you can concentrate on work right now?"

"Well, I figured you would clean that up," I say. "Besides, I've seen worse." I shrug.

He glances at me sideways, as if he's trying to see if I'm joking or not. Unfortunately, I'm not, but I'm not going to elaborate on that with him right now.

"Well, the salon is closed for the day. That's going to take a bit to clean," he says, indicating the puddle on the floor.

"Fine." I cross my arms over my chest. "But you need to figure… that… out." I gesture at the body. "I'll wait here while you do."

"We won't be able to move the body until it gets dark," he says, as if he does this all the time and already knows the drill.

"Okay, well I'll stay here and you come back when it's night-time then. I'll be here waiting. There's plenty of cleaning and admin paperwork to do between now and when you come back."

"No, not happening. I can't just leave you here," he says, shaking his head. "You might run away or call the cops or something. Plus, you've heard my name and you've seen my face. You could identify me in a lineup or whatever, and have one of those drawings made that they put on the news. I can't let that happen."

He does have a fairly unique hairstyle for the island, and that alone would make it easier to track him down. But there's no way I'm sharing that with him. That would just add to his insistence that I can't stay here by myself.

"Listen, I have a vested interest in letting you remove this body and clean up the blood without incident. Do you really think there's a wide audience who like the idea of coming to a murder salon? I'm sure there are some kooks out there who'd get off on it, but not enough to keep a small business afloat and thriving. I need this cleaned up, too, just as much as you do."

He frowns and shakes his head. "No. I mean it. You just watched me murder someone. I'm not going to head out without you and hope for the best."

I roll my eyes.

"Besides," he adds, "you might be tempted to do something stupid like service clients while I'm gone, and then we'll be in trouble."

"Is that what I just did? 'Service' you?" His use of the word makes me feel a little funny, and I feel the need to mention it. Jesus, I just watched him murder someone, there's a body on the floor of my salon, and yet I still have the urge to flirt with him. What is wrong with me?

I feel like maybe what just happened hasn't sunk in. That I'm infusing humor and flirtation rather than facing what just happened head-on. It wouldn't be the first time I've found ways to distract myself from things I don't want to think about.

Hot Guy peers at me for a moment, as if he's trying to read

my mind, and then winks. "No, but I'd like it if you did. Any time you want, Angel, you can service me any way you like. Or any way that I tell you to."

His gaze explores my body, lingering on my chest, and he bites his lower lip.

"You know, we have a little time to kill before it gets dark," he says.

I feel a crackle of electricity and my cheeks flush. I'm tempted to see what he has in mind. But after a moment of gazing back at him, and a dull ache starting in my core, I wrench my eyes away from his gorgeous face.

Instead, I now look at The Asshole's dead mouth, curled up in a scream, blood running from it as well as his gaping neck and throat wounds.

A shiver runs through my entire body as I recognize the air in the salon has taken on the all too familiar sweet and metallic scent of blood. I've been around far too much blood in my lifetime, primarily my own, and it's still a bit of a trigger. I have a little flashback to all the times I've seen it pouring, trickling, oozing from places it shouldn't, both on me and other people.

I watch Hot Guy as he stalks around the body like he's mentally mapping how he's going to dispose of it. His eyes are cold and clinical, and gone is the twinkly, flirtatious, warm guy I was chatting with before The Asshole entered the salon.

Hot Guy's abrupt change in demeanor snaps me out of my trance. This is not the time to flirt, this is not the time to perv at hot men. This is the time to protect myself and get out of a potentially very dangerous situation.

I've just become a witness to a murder. I know who did it, I know what he looks like, his last name, and what he does for work. This knowledge compromises my safety.

The hairs rise on the nape of my neck and my hands grow clammy.

I just watched him kill a man.

I can't let on that I'm scared, so I clear my throat and try to keep my voice calm. "So what, then? Are you going to kill me, too?" I may as well be direct, to know where I stand. To let him know I know he might consider ending my life.

As he shifts his gaze from the dead body to me, I shiver under his stare. His warmth has definitely disappeared. It feels like he's assessing me and my value, both alive and dead. The way he'd maybe assess accepting or turning down a business opportunity.

"I guess we'll have to wait and see," he says, pressing his lips into a firm line, his eyes boring into mine. "And the decision won't be mine alone."

Fuck. I don't even know what that means, but it doesn't sound good. I need to tread carefully here while I figure a way out.

He may be incredibly hot, but he's clearly fucking psychotic.

And he's just killed someone.

If I'm not careful, I'll be next.

CHAPTER 4

AIDAN

The living room TV murmurs quietly in the background, and occasionally pots and pans clatter in the nearby kitchen. Other than that, the place is quiet.

Our compound is a recent acquisition. Business has been doing very well here on the island, and having top-notch security has only become more important.

Success brings a target on your back. We're well aware that several rival groups envy the wealth and power we've accumulated in a very short time here, and we're only getting started.

My business partners and I had visited the island several times over the past decade or so, mainly for pleasure, but we'd also dabbled in the odd business deal and found it worth our while.

It was only around eighteen months ago that we moved from the mainland to make this our home base. We saw an opportunity here to muscle in and stake our claim to some lucrative opportunities that weren't being leveraged by others as well as they could have been.

For whatever reason, this island attracts subpar criminals

with a misplaced sense of right and wrong, their potential to be the best smothered by their arbitrary moral code.

That's the thing about us Brixtons and moral codes. We don't have one and we never will. That's a big reason we're so strong, why we're amassing power here at an exponential rate while others flounder or just stay stagnant.

The compound sits in an industrial neighborhood surrounded by warehouses, factories and storage facilities. On the ground floor is a warehouse that imports items used by restaurants, a cover for the more profitable items we move to and from the island. It's a massive industrial space, full of crates and forklifts and workers scurrying around to get things where they need to go.

We don't just move restaurant equipment and food. We'll move anything, as long as the price is right. Guns, drugs, organs. Even entire people. It's all the same to us, a means to an end. We mainly focus on guns and drugs at the moment, but nothing is off the table and we make that abundantly clear to whoever does business with us. We're a one-stop-shop, and people value our ruthlessness and our commitment to execution.

The top floor of the compound is where the actual business happens. It's a far cry from downstairs, not that anyone who works down there would have the slightest idea.

Up here it's sleek and modern, a soundproof luxury apartment with the best technology. There are high ceilings dangling with elaborate light fixtures, and modern art adorns the walls. A large living room with an oversized U-shaped modular couch and a massive TV with all the latest features. A state-of-the-art kitchen with a massive kitchen island and breakfast in the middle, and a dining room table off to the side. Several bedrooms and bathrooms, an entertainment room, a library, multiple offices and a state-of-the-art fitness center.

And on the other side of the top floor, there are commercial premises that we use as our corporate headquarters. That side of the building features a huge reception desk with a chandelier hanging above it. Sleek office setups with glass desks boast views of the mountains at the back and the ocean in front.

We haven't exactly followed the island motif here. It's cosmopolitan, sophisticated luxury, like we've transported what we were accustomed to on the mainland right into this tropical paradise. Sometimes it's nice to have creature comforts that remind you of home.

In terms of business, besides our import, export and transportation dealings, it helps to have some front-facing operations on the island as well. Being able to get in front of people makes it easier to connect sellers with viable buyers and keep a pulse on the island's activities.

We own three strip clubs in the city and tourist districts, a couple of bars and clubs, and a restaurant with an underground gambling den tucked away in the back. Some of them are more lucrative than others, but all serve a purpose.

I glance over at Brick. He's slouching against the corner of the overstuffed couch across from me, looking deep in thought as he chews on a toothpick. He's wearing his usual black leather jacket and a black and red plaid shirt with dark jeans and red lace-up Converse shoes.

Brick didn't get the memo that we moved to an island. I guess none of us did. It was warm at first, but we've acclimated and stuck with our mainland style. None of us can get down with the idea of wearing shorts, tank tops and flip-flops every day like most other people here do, even when they're working. We're much more comfortable dressing for business. Except for when we're surfing, of course.

When we're in the ocean, it's one of the few times we ever see Brick without his leather jacket. You wouldn't know it to look at it, but it's made of vegan leather. One of the weirdest things about Brick, and there are many, is that he's vegan. Not that being vegan is weird, but being Brick and vegan certainly is. He tortures and kills people for work, getting off on disemboweling and shooting and stabbing. Becoming elated after administering electric shocks and burns and removing fingernails. He enjoys every moment that he gets to torture and maim and kill, and wouldn't trade his job for the world. But apparently, he won't eat an animal.

"Do you think we can trust Tane and his men?" Brick emerges from his daydream, glances up at me and then over to the kitchen where our business partner Slade is cooking.

While they're my business associates, sometimes I'll refer to these guys as my brothers, because we are a brotherhood of sorts, although technically we're not related. We may as well be, having grown up together and now living under the same roof and running an empire.

Besides, we're the closest family any of us have anymore.

"That's like asking if we can trust a vegan with a paint can around a fur coat," calls out Slade from the kitchen, not missing a beat.

He rarely says much, he's just not a big talker for the sake of it. But when he does, it's usually acidic, zinging his target without pause. The topic of Brick being vegan is accepted as fair game for teasing, even by Brick himself.

Slade flicks a saute pan in his right hand and I hear a sizzling sound as the pungent aroma of garlic fills the room. He's a skilled cook, and the kitchen is his refuge, which works for the rest of us in the apartment who can barely boil water.

Brick stares at him, confused. "What the fuck does that mean, bro? And is there meat in that?" He gestures toward the pan Slade is expertly flicking with his wrist.

I smirk. "I believe it means no, Brick, Slade and I don't trust Tane at all. But it's not like we have a choice at the moment. He has too much power over the island chain for us to do much about it. For now, anyway."

"Yeah, that is what it means," Slade nods, "and I'm making you a separate meal, like usual, you picky tree-hugging psychopath."

I snort. That's a pretty accurate description of Brick. He's a psycho with a soft heart when it comes to nature and wildlife. One moment he's strangling a man and threatening to chop off his dick, the next he's patting a bunny and making a wheatgrass smoothie. A real mind fuck, that one.

Brick forms his hands into a heart shape and holds them up to Slade. I snort and roll my eyes. I'm trying to take over an island and two of my key counterparts are over here acting like complete goofballs.

I hate Tane Brown more than just about anyone I've ever met. He essentially rules the islands, controlling who and what comes and goes. He funnels the most profitable opportunities to those he favors, and his connections run deep. Thankfully, his own compound is based on a different island from ours, and he rarely visits, but he still controls things here remotely.

He's an evil man, very strong when it comes to his networks, with a large team of loyal followers who will risk their lives to protect him so they can share in his power. Several groups have tried to overthrow him over the years, but none have succeeded.

"We need to bide our time and strike when the conditions are perfect," I explain. "It's like when you know the waves are going to do exactly what you need them to do. If you rush out an hour beforehand, the waves are going to be too big and crush you. But if you wait until things are just right, until the conditions set you up for success, you can get exactly what you want. You can use them to your advantage and take what's yours."

"I'm getting sick of waiting, though," huffs Brick. "His rules and limitations on us are frustrating. We could be doing so much more. There are better ways to do things here."

"I know, man. But it hasn't been that long, only about eighteen months. We're growing stronger every day. I'm hopeful that we'll reach a point in the next couple of years when we can take him on and have a chance at winning."

"Hope is for the weak, and years are long." Brick juts out his jaw and taps his foot. He cracks his knuckles, his nostrils flared, like he's ready to go and overthrow the islands' primary mafia boss single-handedly. He isn't the most patient person, and sometimes he makes rash decisions. His enthusiasm can have a run-on effect on the rest of the guys. Part of my role is to make sure he and the others don't do anything stupid.

"I will not die at the hands of Tane fucking Brown because we didn't plan things out when you got impatient," I say, glaring at him because I've already explained this many times. "Right now, we would stand no chance unless we formed an alliance, maybe multiple, with other groups here. We'd have to make compromises to partner with them and then find a way to go after him together. And I don't want to weaken our position. We need to be the alpha group if we do end up joining forces, which I really don't want to do. We might be scaling our operations quickly, but it's still early days and we need time to prepare."

Brick takes a deep breath and then lets it out heavily, dropping his shoulders in resignation. He's always chomping at the bit to rush in and start a fight. Or in this case, what would almost certainly be a full-blown, bloody war.

Slade's a little more restrained, more cautious and less of an instigator on his own behalf, but he'll jump in and do anything to help us when any of us need him. If Brick jumps into a situation preemptively, he can end up dragging Slade into unnecessary danger.

Roman, who's out getting yet another haircut, is down for anything that won't mess up his physical appearance. And he's a decently good fighter for a pretty boy.

Besides enjoying women, he also enjoys breaking the odd skull and dominating others physically, and having them submit to his will.

It's on me to pull them all back, having them operate on logic and rationality over instinct and the thrill of the chase. Making sure that our moves are purposeful and thoughtful.

It's on me to keep my brothers alive.

And to make sure we always come out on top.

CHAPTER 5

While the hottie was very flirty immediately after I killed The Asshole, which made my cock twitch, something in the air has shifted now.

I get the sense that she initially blocked out the death part, diverting attention to me while her brain raced to process what had just happened. I'm sure witnessing a murder wasn't what she was expecting during her shift today.

Neither was I, but here we are.

She's panting a little, her ample chest visibly rising and falling and her plush lips parted slightly in a way that makes me want to plunge my tongue deep inside her mouth. Her gorgeous green eyes are wide now as she glances from me to The Asshole's bloody body

Her face is slightly flushed and coated in a gentle sheen, the way I can imagine she looks after she's just been fucked. In fact, everything about her looks like she's turned on by the thrill of what just happened, the sight of this man's blood pooling on the floor. But I also know she's scared.

I must seem like a massive threat to her, and I am, so she'd be right to think that. She doesn't know anything about me other than that I'm more than prepared to kill, to use deadly violence.

She turns as if she's going to walk away from me.

I grab her arm just above her elbow.

She tries to wrench it free, but I increase my grip.

"Let go of me!" she hisses, narrowing her eyes at me through her long, thick lashes, her lower lip jutting out in an angry pout.

Jesus, she's sexy when she's pissed.

She can see I don't have any plans to let her go, so she kicks her leg out at me, aiming for my nutsack. I narrowly manage to avoid her foot and I twist her closer to me so she has less leverage to try to kick me again.

With my hand still on her forearm, I grab her other wrist and pull her close to me.

She hisses in my face and tries to stamp on my foot, but she's too close to get decent leverage and she misses, her leg twisting awkwardly in the air until she places it back on the ground.

I move my hand from her arm to her throat, and I squeeze, cutting off her air supply for a moment, her face just inches from mine. Fear flashes in her eyes, but she immediately regroups and her eyes narrow.

I loosen my grip on her throat, and she hungrily gulps air into her starving lungs.

"Let *go* of me!" She tries to wrestle out of my grip, but I just pull her closer, moving my hand from her wrist and clamping it down just above her elbow.

I squeeze her throat more firmly again, and she fights for breath, but she can't get any air. Her face flushes and her eyes bulge slightly, her face breaking out into a panicked sheen.

She needs to calm down and realize I'm the one in control here, of everything. That I'll let her go if and when I feel like it. That there's no point in trying to run.

I release my grip on her throat, and she gulps in more air.

She glares at me, her chest rapidly rising and falling.

"Are you done now?" I ask her.

She narrows her eyes further.

"If you're going to kill me, just fucking do it. Double the body count," she snarls, glancing over my shoulder at The Asshole's prone corpse. "You're either going to or you're not. There's no need for this little dance, of you cutting off my air supply every five seconds. So if I'm going to die today, do us both a favor and get it out of the way." Her voice rises as she speaks, her agitation growing.

She tries again to yank her arm away from my tight grip, and instead of letting her go, I shove her in her shoulder, spinning her around so her back is to me.

Still firmly gripping her arm, I twist it behind her and push her up against the floor-to-ceiling mirror. The side of her face presses into the glass, and her breath puffs steam against her reflection.

I press my body up against her and dip my head so my mouth is right beside her ear.

"Stop fighting," I growl, my breath whispering across her face, "and lower your voice, because there's a dead body in here and I really don't want anybody to call the cops right now because they heard a hysterical person screaming from the nearby salon."

"Let go of me then," she rasps, her face still pressed against the mirrored wall. "I don't like being held down like this. It makes me panic, and I shout when I'm panicked. So if you want me to be quiet, let me go."

She wriggles in an attempt to get away, and I press closer, my body melding into hers from behind, holding her in position.

"I'll let you go when I want to let you go," I hiss in her ear. "Remember, I'm the one in control here." The back of her ear proves too much to resist, and I run my tongue up the hard piece of cartilage that joins it with her skull.

She jerks her head away and yells, "Fuck you, asshole!"

With all her might, she rears back, smacking the back of her head into my chin and elbowing me in the abdomen. Startled, I jump back and lose my grip on the hand that I've been pressing behind her. She wrenches it free and wheels around to face me. Lowering her center of gravity by bending herself into a squat, she lifts her forearms up in defense and balls up her fists. She tries to dart to my right, but I block her, moving my body into the space.

Panting, she darts to her left and ducks, almost slipping through the gap at my side, but I manage to wrap my arms around her waist from behind and pull her to me. I spin both of us around and move toward the mirrored wall directly in front of us.

My own heart is racing now. I really had to work to get her under my control. She almost slipped through my grasp. For someone her size, for a girl, she's a pretty scrappy fighter. She was never going to win, but fuck, she gave it a good go.

I turn her around so that her back is up against the wall, and my body presses in close to hers so there's no chance she can slip past again. I'm acutely aware of her breasts squeezing against my abdomen.

She emanates anger and heat, her chest rising and falling rapidly as her eyes flit around looking for any options to escape.

"Don't make me hurt you," I growl. "Because I'll need to if you don't cooperate."

"You'd really hurt a girl?" Still breathing heavily, she looks at me through her thick eyelashes and raises her voice to a higher pitch. I know exactly what she's doing, but I'm immune to her manipulation.

She's given me a taste of who she is, and I want more. But I also don't trust her as far as I can throw her. I have the feeling she'd escape in an instant, given a fraction of a chance. She's proven herself wily. Feisty. I like it, but I will not let her get away.

"The way you fight, you give me no choice." I shrug, maintaining eye contact.

She narrows her eyes again.

I let my eyes trail down her face and chest, enjoying the way my body feels pressed into her curves.

"You really are drop-dead gorgeous, by the way." I tilt her chin up with my finger, and her gaze meets mine.

I feel myself getting hard as I take her all in, my erection poking into her stomach. "And the way you fight is hot as fuck."

Her eyes darken, and she bites her bottom lip while she continues to meet my gaze. She doesn't respond verbally, but she doesn't need to. I can tell she's attracted to me, too.

A long moment passes while we just stand here, looking at each other. Not to mention my throbbing hard-on that's digging into the front of her body, wanting to be inside her.

"Let me go," she eventually says, her voice husky. But she makes no move to get away from me.

I dip my face closer to hers, our mouths nearly touching, and know that she can feel my breath on her face. "You don't have a say in this. But I might never want to let you go."

Her chest rises and falls more rapidly now, and her face flushes, her mouth parting slightly, her gaze lowering to my lips. She wants me to kiss her.

I consider it for a moment, but instead of indulging my lips on the kissable pillows that frame her smart mouth, I abruptly pull away.

For a moment, she looks surprised and almost disappointed. But then she glances around the salon, presumably still looking for an escape route. She sighs, clearly not seeing any options.

"Now, are you going to be compliant, or do I need to knock you out?" I ask, my eyes locked on hers. "I can tell you're still looking for ways to get out of here, and that needs to stop."

She glares at me. "Wouldn't you be doing the same if you were in my situation?"

"Yes, but I wouldn't be in your situation." I shrug.

She clenches her jaw and narrows her eyes further. I guess what I said might have been a little condescending.

"Is there a door leading into a back alley here?" I ask, looking around.

"No," she says, but she hesitates for a fraction too long and her eyes involuntarily flicker toward the rear of the salon.

"You just lied to me," I frown at her. "I don't like liars."

"What the fuck do you expect from me right now?" Her voice is shrill, and it echoes around the room's thin walls. I'm increasingly worried she's going to draw attention to the salon and therefore the body of the man I just murdered.

"Be *quiet*," I hiss, glaring at her. I'm getting annoyed now, because she's really starting to put us at risk.

The last thing I need is to be hauled away in handcuffs for dropping the loser whose body lies prone in the middle of the salon. My brothers would work their magic to get me out and any charges dropped, but it would slow down our progress on the business, which we really can't afford.

"Okay, okay," she says, lowering her voice and putting her hands up in mock surrender. "No need to hiss at me."

"I expect you to tell me the truth, Angel," I say, my voice low. I carefully enunciate every syllable because I want no room for misunderstanding. "But you chose to lie to me just now. I asked you to be quiet, but instead, you are choosing to yell. I'm going to make you pay for both of these things. You can trust me on that. You're coming with me, whether you like it or not. And now you've eliminated all of my other options."

I yank The Asshole's gun from my back pocket and raise it high above my head. Her eyes grow large as she looks up at it, and I bring it down forcefully, butt-first, smashing her in the top of her skull.

She crashes to the ground, her head narrowly avoiding the hard edge of a hair-washing basin during her descent. Oops. It looks like it's made of some pretty hard material, and if she hit it hard enough, it could have killed her or at least done some serious damage.

That would have been the last thing I needed. Two dead bodies on my hands, both unexpected.

And in her case, it would have been a real waste. Because she really is gorgeous.

Glancing at her unconscious body crumpled on the ground, I clench my jaw. This could be a really bad idea, but for whatever reason, I've decided not to kill her. I'm taking her with me, back to the house.

I shake my head. Today has been unbelievable. I've murdered some guy with a poor attitude and a trigger finger. Now I've knocked out a hot girl and am going to take her captive because I can't figure out what else to do with her.

And all I wanted was a fucking haircut.

I grab my cell phone out of my pocket and call Aidan and, as usual, he answers on the first ring. Reliable and predictable, no messing around from him. "What?" he says. Also not the height of hospitality when he's on the phone.

"I need your help with something. Bring the others. Now."

"You need help to get your hair cut?" he snorts down the line.

"Stop fucking around. This is serious," I frown. "No questions. Just get here and bring a tarp. I'll text you the details."

He must realize I'm not my usual jokey self. If anything, I'm acting more like him, all business. So he stops with the quips and questions. "Alright man, we'll be right there. Send us the details."

I message them the address and tell them to meet me out in the back alley.

While I wait, I take the opportunity to make sure the blinds are fully closed and double-check the front door is securely locked. I don't want to take any chances with the body just laying there. We don't need some grandma coming in for a blue rinse and a perm right now.

They only take about ten minutes to arrive, announcing their arrival by knocking on the door to the back alley. All three of them come—Aidan, Slade and Brick. Aidan must have recognized the serious tone in my voice when I said to bring everyone. This isn't a two-person job.

Letting them in through the back entrance, they give me strange looks as they pass through the small staff kitchen and enter the main salon. They glance at the bodies and the pool of blood spreading out underneath the man.

"I thought you were just getting a haircut," says Brick, assessing the scene. "But it looks like you had a lot of fun without us."

I shrug. "That was the plan, but I guess he followed me here," I gesture at the body.

Slade walks toward it to take a closer look. "Looks like one of Zero's guys. I've seen him around," he says. I envy his photographic memory, particularly when it comes to assholes trying to take over our business.

"We need to get rid of him, obviously," I say. "I was hoping you guys could help with that."

"And what about her?" Aidan asks, gesturing toward Angel. "You knocked her out?" He inspects her from a distance. "She's not dead?"

"She's alive, and she's coming back with us," I say, as if I've made the executive decision on behalf of all four of us, mentally crossing my fingers that they'll all just go along with it. Even though we've never taken someone captive before and it's kind of a big deal now that I'm thinking about it.

"Like you think we should kidnap her?" Aidan raises an eyebrow. "I don't know if we have time to deal with a prisoner."

"Yeah, that sounds like an awful idea," Slade scowls. "We don't need females getting in the middle of our business."

"Could be fun, though, having a woman around." Brick wiggles his eyebrows.

I might have a reputation as the ladies' man of the group, but the rest of them like women a lot, too. Except for Slade, who's just different. Lots of baggage with that one when it comes to females. Of course, Brick is excited at the prospect of having one in our house to play with.

"Listen. She's got some fight in her," I shrug. "She could be useful to have around."

"So she's not only a prisoner, but a stroppy one who will try to fight us?" Aidan raises an eyebrow.

"Bad idea," says Slade, furrowing his brow. "I'm telling you."

"I can think of some things we could use her for." Brick grins and wiggles his eyebrows again.

Slade rolls his eyes. "Can we think with our brains and not our dicks? *Please.*"

"It feels like we're going around in circles here," I say. "But either way, we need to clean up and get this dead body the fuck out of this salon. And we can't just leave her here."

"Alright, look. I agree we can't just leave her here," says Aidan. "We need to remove her from the scene. Let's bring her with us and then we'll figure out what to do."

"Sounds like a plan," I nod. "We're four powerful guys and she's just one woman. What could possibly go wrong?"

CHAPTER 6

AIDAN

"Ro, go get your car and drive it around back. And then you two dispose of that," I say to Roman and Slade, gesturing at The Asshole's body. "Brick, you and I will deal with the girl."

"Sure, I'll help to clean up Roman's mess as usual," says Slade, rolling his eyes. He might be protesting at my instructions, but I know he'll still follow them.

After Roman retrieves his vehicle from the front of the strip mall and drives it around the back of the building, I pick the girl up from the ground and haul her over my shoulder.

Brick follows me, grabbing her purse from a hook on a coat stand in the break area.

I carry her outside, and he closes up, locking the back exit.

He opens the door to the back seat of the car and I place her inside so that she's lying down on her back.

The other guys wrap The Asshole's body in a tarp, and then silently carry it over to their car and throw him in the trunk. They know what to do. Even though today's events were unexpected, it's not entirely out of the ordinary having someone coming to fuck with us, and us needing to teach them a permanent lesson. It's just how it is around here. It's just business.

While I drive, Brick digs around in the girl's purse and retrieves an ID.

"Angel Benson," he reads aloud. "248 White Oak St, Apt 3."

I nod and type it into the GPS.

"Also, I've never seen so many box cutter knives and pepper spray canisters outside of a hardware store," he says, rummaging around in her purse and pulling some out to show me. "We should watch out when she wakes up." He grins as he extends the sharp blade on a box cutter and inspects it. "I like a girl who knows her way around a knife."

I shake my head and roll my eyes. Brick is obsessed with weapons and women separately, but together they're his kryptonite. If they have tattoos and piercings, even better.

Glancing at the sharp blade in his hand, maybe he's right. We *should* watch out when she wakes up. For all we know, she's a complete lunatic. Who knows what she's capable of?

After driving for about half an hour, the GPS signals that we've reached our destination. We pull up at a dilapidated apartment building on the outskirts of the city.

Without going in, I already know a lot about this place. I grew up somewhere just like this. It's not a good part of town, with lots of sketchy activity going on at all hours of the day.

An air of hopelessness and decay emanates from the grungy gray building that would probably never look clean even if someone water-blasted it for days. It's like the human despair hiding inside is leaching out into the architecture, exposing it for the world to see.

Or maybe I'm just projecting.

By the look of the building, it's going to be easy for Brick to get in without a key, and there's guaranteed not to be any high level of security, maybe none at all. Not that it would matter. Brick is talented at getting into most structures when he wants to, the slippery fuck.

From what I know of buildings like this, it's probably unsafe for a woman to live here by herself with its flimsy locks, questionable onsite activities and lack of security. Although judging by Roman's tousled appearance earlier, which for once didn't come about because he just fucked someone, it looks like she gave him a run for his money, and that she's fairly capable of defending herself.

"You go in," I say to Brick. "I'll stay here with the girl."

"You going to have some fun with her while she's knocked out?" Brick grins at me and wiggles his eyebrows, pretending to squeeze his pecs as though they were breasts.

"No, of course I'm fucking not." I narrow my eyes at him. "Jesus. Just go get a bunch of her clothes and whatever other shit she might need. Makeup and shoes. Underwear. Tampons. Hair ties. Whatever it is that women need."

"How long is she going to stay with us, man?"

"I don't know. Just get a bunch of stuff and put it in a bag. It's not as if we planned today in advance, so I haven't really thought about how long she might stay. I'm not sure what Roman was even thinking, getting us to take her with us. But we needed to get rid of the body and couldn't just leave her there. Seemed a bit rash to kill her on the spot."

"I would have," smirks Brick. He glances at the girl. "Even though she's really pretty."

"Yeah, well, you're a fucking psycho."

"Samesies," he says, pointing at me, grinning as he slams the passenger door closed. He spins around on the ball of his foot and walks away from the vehicle. He slips into the darkness and heads toward the apartment listed on her ID.

I wait for five, then ten, then fifteen minutes and Brick still hasn't come back. I sigh and roll my eyes. He's probably busy sniffing her panties and jerking off.

There's a soft moan from the back seat. Shit. She's starting to wake up already. Roman mustn't have hit her hard enough.

It's always a delicate balance, bashing someone in the head

forcefully enough so that they're rendered unconscious, without permanently damaging their brain. I've seen Brick blow through that threshold a few times with people that deserved it.

I turn some music on, loud enough to create some cover, but also not so loudly that it draws undue attention to the vehicle.

She groans again, louder this time, and her arms reach up to rub her groggy eyes. Poor thing, she's going to have a splitting headache soon if she doesn't already.

"Wh—where the fuck am I?" She narrows her eyes at me as they adjust to the moonlight. "And who the fuck are you?"

"Hi there, Angel," I say, letting a small smile play across my face. "Nice to meet you."

She sits up and groans, looking around. She tries the door handle on her left side, but of course, it's locked. Tugging at it some more, she glares at me. "Let me the fuck out!"

"That's not going to happen, Angel," I shrug.

"How do you know my name?"

"Magic." I grin, and she narrows her eyes at me.

She peers out the window and her eyes light up as she recognizes the building. "We're at my apartment! Let me out!" She tugs at the door again.

"Angel, the door isn't going to open. You're not going to your apartment. You're coming with us. My buddy is just getting some of your things, so you can be more comfortable."

"To go where?" She stops talking for a moment, as if she's trying to process what I just said. "Wait, seriously though. Who the fuck are you? Where's the guy from the salon?"

"He's… tending to an errand."

She peers at me, and then recognition dawns in her eyes. "Fuck, is he getting rid of The Asshole's body?"

I laugh. "If you mean the guy he killed back there, then yes. That's what he's doing."

"Thank goodness for that. It's really off-putting for customers to have a corpse just laying there while their hair gets cut. I was worried he was just going to leave it there." She winces and grabs the side of her head. "By the way, I have a really nasty headache and it hurts like hell. Is that courtesy of your friend, too?"

"Yeah. Sounds like you deserved it though." I grab a small bottle of water and a travel pack of over-the-counter pain relief and pass them back to her. "Here you go."

She snatches the items out of my hands and unscrews the water bottle. For a moment, I think she's going to throw its contents all over me, but she seems to change her mind. She opens the pain relief packet and uses the water to wash the two tablets down.

"So, are you going to tell me where you're taking me?" She glares at me in the rear-view mirror.

"You'll find out in good time. Be patient."

"You try being fucking patient when you wake up in the back seat of a car with a stranger outside your apartment. After witnessing a fucking murder in your workplace!" Her voice is rising, and I need her to shut up. Not that I think the people who live in this apartment building are necessarily the types that would call the cops for any type of help.

"I need you to calm down, Angel. Stop yelling, please." I keep my voice calm, hoping it will rub off on her.

"Or what?"

"Or there'll be a repeat of what happened to you earlier."

"What? You're saying you'll knock me out, too?"

"If I have to, yes," I shrug.

"Fuck you!" she yells. "Let me out of this car!"

I'm not worried about anybody seeing what's happening inside the vehicle, because the windows are heavily tinted and it's dark outside. But I am a little concerned about someone hearing her yell. I turn up the music a little more.

"So, Angel, what do you do when you're not waking up in cars with strange men?"

She crosses her arms across her chest. "I eat guys like you for breakfast," she fumes. "You're making a big mistake holding me like this."

"Oh really? What are you going to do about it? Because so far, from what I know, things haven't been going so well for you."

She reaches over and bops me on the head with the empty water bottle. It makes a hollow sound and bounces off my head and out of her hand, landing on the passenger seat.

I snort at her. "That all you've got?"

She tries to reach around the seat and punch my arm.

"I really wouldn't try that, sweetheart." I smile at her as condescension drips from my tongue. "You remember what happened when you tried that with my brother last time, don't you?"

Her eyes narrow. "He got so turned on his dick pressed against my stomach, from what I recall," she snarls. "And then he fucking *knocked me out* apparently, and then *kidnapped* me! Who the fuck are you guys anyway, except obvious assholes?"

"According to my brother, the guy he killed at your salon was an asshole. Is that right, Angel? Didn't you just call him that, too?"

"Fine. Yes, he was an asshole. The Asshole. That's what I called him. I'll call you something else instead. What's your name, anyway?"

I smirk. "My name is Aidan."

"Alright, then, *Aidan," she narrows her eyes and glares at me in the rear-view mirror.* "You're a bad person, I can tell. I know you do bad things. You're like an evil demon."

I smirk and look her dead in the eye. "I can live with being called a demon. You'll come to learn that I'm much worse than that. And before long, I'll have you doing whatever I say. You're under my control now, Angel."

Her eyes grow dark and narrow, her pupils transforming into tiny pinpoints.

I watch in the mirror as she rears her hand back and balls it into a fist, then attempts to crash it through the space between the seats and hit me in the head. Reaching my opposite arm over, I block her with ease, even though the power of her punch is impressive for someone her size, especially given the cramped confines of the vehicle. I laugh as I deflect her fist, and she narrows her eyes further.

She punches at me again with her other arm this time. I dodge her with my body and reach out a hand to stop her. It's tricky to maneuver in the small space and while I deflect her wild blow from my face, I feel a sting as momentum crashes her hand down on me and her sharp nails scratch me through my shirt.

"Putting your nails on me already, baby?" I grin at her. "I like that. Maybe one day you'll rake them over my back and make me bleed while I fuck you senseless."

"More like I'll fucking scratch your eyes out with them," she hisses. "I'll fucking kill you."

She grabs hold of each of the front seats and tries to launch her whole body through the gap, and I laugh, grabbing her by the throat and holding her steady in limbo between the front and back of the vehicle. She tries to gulp in air as my fingers clamp down, cutting off her supply, but it comes out like a dry croak.

"I'm stronger than you, Angel. You might be beautiful, but I'm physically much superior. And I'm a killer. Just like my brothers. We're all capable of that. You've seen it for yourself. Just remember that." I pause and lock eyes with her in the rearview mirror again. "Now forgive me for what I'm about to do."

Using my free hand, I remove my gun from my pocket and raise it up high. Her eyes grow wide as she watches me smash the butt of it down on the top of her head, and she crumples between the seats, knocked out for the second time today.

Some people never learn. But then again, I haven't had a chance to train her yet.

As I inspect her crumpled form, Brick knocks on the passenger door and I let him in. He hops in and sees her slumped over the middle console. "Having some fun while I was up there in her apartment, were you?" he grins.

"The fun is just getting started, brother," I smirk. "What the fuck took you so long, anyway? Did you try on all of her clothes or something? Jerk off in her bed?"

"The place was a mess, man. She had shit everywhere. Had to make sure I grabbed a bit of everything."

He looks slightly suspicious to me, avoiding eye contact like he's hiding something, but I'll let it go for now. We need to get her back to the compound before she wakes up again. We've already knocked her out twice today and a third could be bad for her gorgeous skull.

We silently move her so that she's lying across the back seat again rather than dangling partway into the front of the vehicle.

As we drive back to our compound, I consider her fate.

While the eventual outcome might be us killing her, because she is a murder witness after all, we've gone through all this effort to bring her with us.

Killing or damaging her too badly right now would seem like a waste. A sunk cost. We need some type of return on investment.

She's lucky I'm stubborn like that.

CHAPTER 7

ANGEL

I wake with a start and immediately know I'm somewhere I've never been before. It's not entirely unusual for me to wake up in a strange location, but this time I know it's different.

For one, I glance to either side and there's no random guy snoring next to me. I have a feeling there's nobody in the kitchen making me coffee or breakfast in bed, either, like in a romantic movie.

My skull is also thumping and my mouth is bone-dry, and I'm sitting up with my back against the wall.

It's dark in this room, but the eyelashes on one of my eyes are crusted together and by the familiar metallic smell I assume that it's blood. I try to lift my hand so I can assess the damage by touch, but my arms are restrained behind me somehow. Whatever's holding them feels cold against my wrists rather than something like a rope. It doesn't feel like I'm on a bed, either. The surface I'm on is a little springy, but it seems thin, and like I'm only slightly elevated from the floor.

An image flashes into my head of being in a vehicle and

trying to fight someone. I vaguely recall my vision receding until everything went black. And now apparently I'm here, wherever this is.

It wasn't that fucker from the salon, though. Not the Hot Guy who killed The Asshole. I remember him and what happened there.

The person in the car was another guy, also hot, but different. Aidan, I think he said his name was. He must have brought me here.

I'm assuming that the Aidan guy and Hot Guy know each other, but I'm not sure what I'm basing that on. Just a hunch. Or maybe I'm just linking them together because they're both good-looking, like all good-looking guys are part of some secret gang. Sounds like a gang I'd like to get to know. *Focus, Angel.* Jesus.

My eyes are adjusting to the darkness of this chilly space. The room I'm in is a concrete rectangle with wooden steps ascending to an unknown destination. The floor is hard cement, with a floor drain in the corner. Bare beams and insulation are exposed where a ceiling would normally be. It doesn't take a rocket scientist to guess this is probably a basement.

Lining one wall is a row of lockable cabinets. One has been left open, its double doors spread wide, leaving its contents on display. Various tools are hung neatly on hooks, and the more details I notice, the more I get the sense these guys aren't just into home decorating. Hooks and blades, some that appear to be very sharp and others serrated, everything with a sinister quality that doesn't spell casual weekend wallpapering. I shiver as my eyes rest on something that looks like a branding iron.

Looking down, I can now see I'm sitting on a thin mattress with some strange stains on it. I prefer not to think about what they might be, but there's a definite possibility they're bodily fluids. I fight the urge to wretch. There's no need to add vomit to the existing mess.

I try to squeeze my wrists out of the shackles that keep me attached to the wall, but there's no wiggle room. I'm firmly stuck in place, helpless, with a ton of questions racing through my mind.

Who the fuck are the men that brought me to this room?

Why was The Asshole after Hot Guy at my salon?

Who is Aidan from the car and how does he know Hot Guy?

Why do they keep knocking me out, and why am I here?

CHAPTER 8

SLADE

"Did you dispose of everything okay?" Aidan asks, glancing from me to Roman. We just got back to the compound after leaving the hair salon and taking a long drive out west with the body in the trunk.

"Yeah, we broke it down, bagged it up and buried it in the woods. Found a good deserted spot far from where we left the other ones. We should be good."

We have a few 'regular' spots to leave bodies. There are many untouched locations on the island—forests, rivers, and lakes. It's safer to mix things up rather than create a mass burial site that someone might stumble upon.

"Good," Aidan nods, steepling his fingers under his chin. "Now we just have to figure out what to do with the girl."

"Where'd you put her?" I glance around but don't see any signs of her, which is a relief. I'm half-surprised the guys don't have her laying on a sun lounger while they fan her and feed her grapes, the horny fucks.

"She's down in my special room," grins Brick.

"We're just going to keep her shackled down in the basement?" Roman raises an eyebrow.

"It's out of the way. She'll be less of a distraction down there," I reply.

"But that's no fun." Roman narrows his eyes at me. "And it's not like you're distracted by women."

"I'm not, but the rest of you are. Especially you." I glare back at him.

"We didn't bring her here for fun, Roman," says Aidan. "If you recall, you chose to bring her here because she saw you murder someone."

"The two don't have to be mutually exclusive, you know," Roman wiggles his eyebrows. "Murder witness. Sexy concubine. She could be both."

"She is really sexy," nods Brick. "Such a pretty wee captive."

"I have a feeling she'll end up being more like a succubus," I sigh at him. "Look, you really need to learn to stop thinking with your dick. It's going to get us in trouble one of these days. It already almost has on countless occasions."

"I've always wanted to bang a succubus," says Brick, grinning. "Sounds like a good time!"

"Fuck you're weird, man!" I roll my eyes, and Aidan snorts.

Despite our differences, we're all in agreement with one thing, and that's that Brick is a weird dude. We love him, but he's got some strange ideas.

"I'm okay with her being down in my special room, though," says Brick. "It's almost like she's my pet, waiting for me there. I want to show her all the things I can do with my tools. Maybe I'll find some prey and bring it back just to show her my skills."

"She's not yours. Not your pet," snaps Roman, narrowing his eyes at Brick. "I found her."

"See?" I say to Aidan, gesturing toward Roman and Brick. "She's been here for five minutes and she's already causing conflict, even when she's shackled to the wall in the fucking basement. This is an awful idea, and it's going to rip us apart." I glare at Roman. "There are easier ways to get pussy. I don't know why you're so pressed on her."

"It didn't feel right, killing her there in the salon," he shrugs. "Does it help that she's fucking hot? Sure. But I still wouldn't have snuffed her out there, even if she wasn't."

I'm skeptical about what Roman would have done if she didn't look the way they say she does, but there's no point pressing this now.

My main concern is what having a gorgeous woman under our roof is going to do to our business and our brotherhood.

We have a lot to do if we're going to continue to scale. Rivals are constantly popping up on the island, trying to take over our turf.

Recently, we did a deal with a group of guys who have some type of protection role on this island. Before we came to an arrangement, they'd been a thorn in our side, slowing our profits because of their stupid rules. But we were able to help them free their girl from Tane Brown and his men, and now they owe us. Now they have a window of time to pay off their debt to us, and during that timeframe, they can't fuck with our business the way they usually do.

It's more important than ever that all four of us are laser-focused so that we can ramp and scale before the window closes again and things go back to normal.

Some of our rivals have been a case in point. In their cases, a woman was a distraction, and now their businesses are suffering greatly as a result. Groups like us are benefiting from their weakness and their poor decisions. They're hemorrhaging money because they chose to prioritize and save some random women's lives. They chose love over profit, and look where it's got them.

I just hope this woman we kidnapped today doesn't end up being our downfall, too.

CHAPTER 9

ANGEL

hear footsteps descending the steps toward me. Out of the darkness, a burly man enters the room where I'm shackled to the wall. He's tall and extremely muscular. He wears a red and black shirt rolled up to his elbows, revealing tattooed forearms, and long dark pants with Chuck Taylors that make me want to go back to the eighties when they were originally on trend.

His hair is a dirty blonde, tied back in a ponytail, and he has a scruffy beard.

His eyes are a piercing blue-gray, like the ocean during a windstorm, and his skin is tanned golden. Like his buddy from the salon, I get the feeling he spends a lot of time in the ocean. He's like a sexy tattooed lumberjack surfer, and I am here for it.

I rip my eyes away. *Pull yourself together. You're shackled to the wall in some random basement full of torture implements, not at a restaurant for a first date. He's obviously insane.*

Trying to come out swinging and to put him on the back foot, figuratively at least, I narrow my eyes at him. "Who the fuck are you?" I ask, my raised voice bouncing off the basement walls.

He glances at me, a half-smirk on his face. "Hey pretty lady," he says. "Nice to meet you. They call me Brick."

"Brick?" I raise an eyebrow.

"Yep, like the thing you build houses with." He shrugs.

"Why? Did your parents not like you?"

He smirks at me. "If I tell you, I'll have to kill you."

My eyes involuntarily dart toward the open locker with all the torture implements neatly displayed on hooks. He could definitely kill me with several of the items. A shiver runs down my spine as I look at some of the sharp blades.

"It's okay. Just don't ask me why my nickname is what it is and you'll be fine." He winks at me and then follows my gaze to the open locker. "Oh, don't worry about those, for now at least. I save them for people who insist on understanding the reason for my nickname."

I'm not sure whether to laugh at his torture jokes or stay completely still, so I freeze in some type of half-smile.

"It's okay, Angel is it? I'm not going to bite, today anyway. I'm going to give you some time to settle in. But after today, all bets are off."

This time I smirk.

"Why am I here?" I ask. "Why am I shackled to a fucking wall in the middle of a basement, sitting on a thin-ass mattress that appears to be coated in some combination of vomit and blood and piss and shit and probably semen and god knows what else?"

His eyes flit to the mattress and he pulls a face as if he's realizing how filthy it is for ht first time.

"Oh, Angel. Don't play dumb. You witnessed a murder. And we can't have you running around telling everyone, can we? And now that you mention it, you've seen a bit more of my basement than I intended you to. I should have kept those lockers closed. Now there are two reasons we can't just let you go."

I feel the color drain from my face, and my lip trembles involuntarily. I jut my jaw out to steady it, and blink hard to hold back the tears that are trying to free themselves from my tear ducts.

Brick glances again at the filthy mattress I'm sitting on and its many stains, and then he looks at me. "There's no semen down here, by the way. I get turned on by the things I do down here, but I haven't jerked off on any of my victims. Then again, I have had no one nearly as attractive as you down here before."

His eyes devour me, trailing over my body and taking me all in, but in a way that makes me feel pretty despite the dingy surroundings. It's like he's admiring my every angle, memorizing my lines. Except I get the funny feeling that instead of analyzing my anatomical contours for a painting or sculpture, he's thinking about where he'd slice me with his scalpel.

As he gazes at me, he steps back, crossing his arms and putting one hand up to his mouth as if he's deep in thought. "Shackling you to the wall and making you sit in this filth, in my house of horrors, doesn't seem fitting, especially for someone as beautiful as you. I want to spend time with you down here, don't get me wrong. There are so many fun activities we could do together, so many things I want to show you. But not right now, not like this."

Removing a key from his pants pocket, he moves toward me and kneels sideways between me and the fixture attaching the shackles to the wall.

As he gets within inches of my body, I flinch and look down at the floor. His figure is imposing, and I can't wrench myself free from my restraints. I'm completely at his mercy.

"Relax, Angel," he says softly, tipping my chin with his hand so I have no choice but to look right at him, our faces so close I can feel his warm breath. "You deserve somewhere nicer than my torture basement."

He unlocks the clasps that bind me, and as he frees my wrists are I lower my hands, shaking them to get the circulation going again.

He reaches out and clasps one of my forearms in his large,

powerful hand. He pulls me to my feet and tugs me across the basement and up the stairs. "Come on, my beautiful Valkyrie. We're getting you a proper room."

"What did you call me?"

"My Valkyrie. You're my little angel of death."

What a weirdo.

"Are you meant to be doing this? Letting me out of here?" As he leads me away from the disgusting mattress, I raise an eyebrow. I feel like I need a thousand showers after sitting on that, and my skin crawls at the thought of what might have been living on it. I really hope wherever he's taking me is better than this, or at least clean.

"I prefer to ask for forgiveness than permission." He grins. "Besides, you're hardly going to be able to roam free. You're still our captive, after all."

He motions for me to be quiet as we reach the top of the basement stairs and emerge into what seems to be an apartment. We briefly pop out into an open-plan kitchen and dining area with hardwood floors, and he leads me through a short corridor and then up some stairs. We walk along another longer carpeted hallway lined with rooms until we get to a door near the back of the house.

He opens the door and leads me inside. It's a spacious bedroom, and I'm assuming it's a guest room because it doesn't look lived in. It's more like a display you'd find in a model home, sleek and modern, the sheets and walls sparkling white. The bed looks freshly made, and there isn't much personality in here, just some generic modern art. Two nightstands flank the bed, and there's a large dresser on the wall opposite the bed.

At the back of the room are two doors. Brick shows me that one is an ensuite with a shower bath and a basin, and the other is a spacious walk-in closet. Not that I have anything to put in there.

After showing me around, Brick turns to me. "I need to go now, but this suits you much better than my basement. We'll spend some time down there together later, though. I want to show you all the things I can do. You might like it so much you want to join me, try out a few tools yourself."

I shiver as I recall the contents of the closet he'd left open down there.

"Thank you?" I say, my voice tipping up at the end like a question, because I'm not sure why he's doing this for me and I'm still confused about why I'm here at all. But this is a damn sight better than being shackled in the chilly basement full of torture implements.

"I'll see you later," says Brick. He pats my hand and then slips out of the room, closing the door behind him. I hear a lock click into place and his footsteps retreat down the hallway.

Waiting a minute or so, I tiptoe over to the door and turn the handle just in case, but, as expected, it's locked.

I try the window that faces the backyard, but that's locked, too. Through the large glass pane, I can see a small yard below. Tall trees line the yard, blocking out the view of any neighbors.

Although this is better than being in the basement, I still feel claustrophobic. I was trapped down there, and now I'm trapped up here. Still a captive, just more comfortable with a real mattress and pillows.

I flop onto the bed, alone with my thoughts, wondering what's next.

CHAPTER 10

AIDAN

"You did *what*?" Slade glares at Brick. "That's not good. What were you thinking?"

"Slade was right about this whole thing. This doesn't seem like a good idea," I sigh, resting my elbow on the countertop and running my fingers through my hair. Three of us are sitting on chrome high-top chairs at the marble breakfast bar while Slade cooks a meal.

The other guys tease me for being overly cautious, but I prefer dead ends to loose ones.

"At the very least, she's going to be a distraction. And we definitely don't need those right now, with what's going on in the business. This is a critical time for us."

"Listen, like I said, I think we should keep her around for a while," shrugs Roman. "See if she can be of any use to us. Sometimes having a female around could come in handy, especially one that knows how to fight. And besides, you helped bring her here."

I narrow my eyes at him. "Yeah, because I didn't trust you boneheads to handle it. She would have almost certainly run away if you'd been in charge of transporting her, and then we'd have a witness to hunt down."

Roman glares at me. He hates it when I point out his incompetence. But he's the reason we have some feisty lunatic woman under our roof.

"How the hell could she be useful to us, Ro? Is she going to kick us in the nuts? Slit our throats while we're sleeping?" Slade glares at Roman. "It's great that she's good at fighting, but that means she's just as likely to fight *us*. That's the last thing we need to be worrying about."

"I wouldn't mind if she kicked me in the nuts," grins Brick, his eyes twinkling.

"Is that why you freed her from the basement and gave her a proper bedroom?" Slade crosses his arms over his chest. "In hopes that she'd think you were her hero and indulge in all your kinks as a thank you?"

"No. That's not the only reason why," huffs Brick.

"I still think we can have at least a little fun with her before we decide she's more trouble than not," says Roman, shrugging and turning to lock eyes with me. "Maybe she can help relieve some of your pent-up stress, Aidan. Because clearly, you need someone to loosen you up."

I cross my arms and roll my eyes at him, my lip curling slightly at his words.

He glances at Slade. "I'd say the same for you, but we all know you're a lost cause."

Slade's eyes narrow at Roman while he chops meat with a sharp cleaver and throws the chunks into a large pot.

"Slade's managing the situation just fine. You're the one who seems to be obsessed with fucking her," I say, looking at Roman. "So do you, Brick." I turn my attention to the bearded vegan psycho. "By the way, I saw you stuffing those panties in your pocket when you brought her bags of clothing and stuff into the house."

Brick shrugs but doesn't offer any defense against the allegation because it's true. "The only one who doesn't want to fuck her is Slade, because he never wants to fuck anyone anymore," he says, gesturing at Slade whose face remains expressionless. We all know that he isn't completely abstinent, still has a bit of fun now and then. But he just hasn't been the same since his ex betrayed him in the worst way.

"So I don't want her here. Brick and Roman clearly do." Slade stops what he's doing in the kitchen and crosses his arms over his chest. "Where do you stand on this, Aidan?"

I'm not quite ready to throw her out yet, or worse. I'm usually so careful that I wouldn't risk something like this, having a captive in our home, especially someone who has information that could hurt us. But there's something about her I can't quite put my finger on. I need to know more before I can decide.

"Listen, I'll try to break her down a bit and we can go from there," I say, and I can't help a hungry smile from forming on my lips. "I owe her a little talking to for her behavior in the car earlier. Trying to attack me and whatnot."

"Oh, so *you* get to play with the girl and then we'll decide what happens to her? Potentially like a catch and release?" Brick frowns.

"No, it's not like that. I have plans to show her that her behavior hasn't been acceptable. She'll hopefully get in line after what I have planned for her. Although with what I'm planning on doing to her, she might act up just so that I do it again." My cock twitches in anticipation of her punishment. I'm going to take it slowly and enjoy every moment.

"Not fair. I want to play with her too," Brick pouts and crosses his arms tightly over his muscular chest. He looks ridiculous, like some muscly bearded man-child, and I shake my head and laugh.

"I found her first, bro," Roman snaps at Brick. He glares at me. "You always take over everything. If anyone gets to play with her, it should be me."

"Hey, I cleaned up your mess and now I get to enjoy the spoils of my labor," I grin back at him.

Slade says nothing. He just continues to clean the kitchen, but his wiping of the counters becomes more aggressive, his face set into even more of a scowl than usual.

It's clear he doesn't want her here, and he doesn't have the same carnal interest in her that the rest of us do. But that's just how Slade is these days, ever since he lost his love. None of us push him to get over it and move on. He'll change when he's ready and if he wants to, and it has no negative impact on our business. He just rarely gets his dick wet, and he hates all females. No biggie.

I, on the other hand, have a punishment to dish out to our sexy little captive. And I can't wait to see how far I can get her to go until she breaks. Until she submits to me and admits that I'm the one in control.

By the end of our little session, she's going to be screaming my name.

By the end of our little session, I'm going to have a better idea of whether she's someone we'll risk keeping around for a bit longer.

But first, I'm going to lay a trap so the punishment can be even more brutal.

CHAPTER 11

ANGEL

wake to a sound, a loud click, or maybe I'm imagining things. It seems I dozed off on the bed.

I'm lying on my stomach, my face squished into the pillow. It's a comfortable mattress and the pillows are heavenly. Much better than that mess in the basement.

Hopping off the bed, stripped down to the tank top and hot pants I wore underneath my shirtdress, I pad over to the door and try turning the handle. I'm not sure why I'm bothering, given they say the definition of insanity is doing the same thing over and over and expecting a different result. But here I am, insane, expecting the door to be locked but trying it, anyway.

I press down on the handle, waiting to feel resistance, but surprisingly, it keeps turning until the latch pops open with a satisfying ping.

I push the door open, bracing myself for it to squeak and alert everyone that I'm escaping the confines of this room, but the hinges are well-oiled and it silently swings outward.

Peering out into the hallway, I don't see anybody, so I exit the room and tiptoe across the carpet, careful to stick to the edges in case a floorboard creaks. The foundations in this place seem more sturdy than the ones back at my apartment, or anywhere I've ever lived, but it's still a habit to try to slip by silently, to not draw unnecessary attention to myself from people who might hurt me.

Tiptoeing down the stairs, I eye the front door through the kitchen and living room and down an entrance hallway. As I reach the bottom of the stairs, I suddenly feel eight eyes on me.

There's Hot Guy from the salon and the one I have memories of in the car, Aidan. And then Brick, the burly guy who brought me up from the basement to the new room. And another guy, tall and muscular, who seems to be cooking something in the kitchen.

From where I'm standing, I glance at each of them. They're all ridiculously attractive. Four hot, tall, muscular men, their attention focused entirely on me. I still don't know what I'm doing here, but I don't mind the scenery.

"Well, well, well. If it isn't Sleeping Beauty," grins Hot Guy from the salon. The hot murderer that I saw kill someone. That probably has a lot to do with why I'm here, now that I think about it. In fact, it's kind of shocking that I'm still alive after what I saw yesterday.

"Well, well, well. If it isn't Mr. Come Into Your Workplace and Kill Someone and Kidnap You Guy," I reply, deadpan.

The others glance at each other and laugh.

"Who said you could leave your room, Angel?" Aidan arches an eyebrow at me.

"Nobody said I couldn't," I reply, placing my hand on my hip. "Last I looked, I was a grown-ass woman who could make decisions about where to go in this world."

"That was before you became a witness to a murder," Aidan shrugs. "That carries responsibilities. You've become a liability, and you have to do what we say now."

"The door was also unlocked, so I walked out of it," I shrug.

"It shouldn't matter if we have removed the door from its

hinges and there's just air keeping you between the room and the hallway, Angel. You're under our control, and you need to do exactly as we say. If you're told to stay in your room, you need to stay there."

"Because you said so? I'm not under your control." I glare at him. He's treating me like a dog who's being trained to sit and stay when there's a treat sitting right in front of it. But in this case, the treat is my freedom. "Why are you such a jerk, anyway? You're so controlling. I remember how you behaved in the car, and now this. Fuck you, asshole!"

"Oh, you're going to regret talking to me that way, sweetheart," Aidan's voice is calm, but it drips with condescension.

"I am *not* your sweetheart!" I narrow my eyes at him. What a prick.

"Keep going, and watch the punishment get more severe," shrugs Aidan, his eyes glimmering at me as if he's planning something truly cruel.

"A punishment? Really? How innovative of you." I roll my eyes.

"Watch it," he says, his tone changing from amusement to a warning.

"Or what?" I raise an eyebrow.

"Or I will make you ride the line between pleasure and pain so hard you'll never think about another man again."

Okay. This changes things. My pussy clenches. I wonder what he has in mind and I can't wait to see. "Is that a threat or a promise?"

"Can't it be both?"

"I dare you to punish me." I jut my chin out in what I hope comes across as defiance. He clearly wants control, and I will not let him just take it. If he wants to punish me, I'm going to make him really punish me.

He shakes his head. "I don't think you could take it."

"I bet you I can." I've never been able to resist a dare or a bet.

"Fine. But you need to tell me you're sure that you want

everything I'm going to dish out to you," he says, his eyes locked with mine, his expression serious. "Because this will be painful. Your body is going to be screaming and spent by the end."

"Even better." I maintain eye contact, my body tingling in anticipation at his words.

"Oh, you like pain?" His eyes grow dark and he once again lets them trail over me as if he's planning my punishment out in his mind.

"It all depends on the circumstances, the setting, and whether there's pleasure involved, too."

"Alright, well you're literally asking for it," he smirks, his gaze unwavering, "so I'm going to give it to you as requested." He diverts his gaze to the kitchen, where the guy I haven't spoken with is standing. "But let's have dinner first. Slade made us a nice meal, didn't you, Slade?"

I glance over at the guy in the kitchen. Slade, I guess. He's scowling at me.

"Oh, you've both realized you're not the only two people in the room?" he smirks and shakes his head. "I told you she'd be a distraction. You were so focused on her you almost forgot to eat, Aidan."

Aidan glares at Slade.

I can tell that Slade dislikes me and doesn't want me to be here. It's palpable.

"Why are you glaring at me like that? You don't even know me. I have done nothing to you and I didn't ask to be here." I narrow my eyes at him.

"Don't take it personally," says Brick. "Slade hates all women."

"Yeah," says Slade, his eyes narrowing at me in what appears to be disgust. "You're nothing special."

CHAPTER 12

ANGEL

The five of us seat ourselves around the dinner table.

Ordinarily, I'd describe the table as large. It's sleek and modern, like the rest of the furniture in this place, made up of solid woodgrain planks, and looks like it would seat about six normal people. But with this group, it's a tight squeeze. Four tall and muscular guys and me, crowded around the slab of wood. It's cozy, but we make do.

I'm sitting between Slade and Roman, each of us in our own plush black boucle chairs. The seats are comfortable with curved backs, and I lean into the backrest, sinking into the softness. I don't know that any of these guys have an eye for interior design, but if someone picked the furniture out, I think it would have been Aidan or Roman.

Aidan, because he likes to control everything down to the last detail.

Roman because he'd want everything to look perfect in his den of seduction.

Maybe I'm wrong. Maybe Slade has an eye for design, and his grumpiness just overshadows his artistic side. He is pretty creative with his cooking, judging by the attention he seemed to be putting into cooking dinner.

It's definitely not Brick who picked out the furniture, though. That's for sure. I've only known him for a moment, but can tell he largely reserves his creativity for torture. That's what lights him up, gets his juices flowing. And, if he was to dabble in interior design, his aesthetic would be much more gothic, with skulls and crosses and lots of red and black detailing.

Aidan sits across from me and Brick is over to the left of Slade, at the end of the table. It would have made more sense for Roman to sit at the other end, across from Brick, but when I sat down, he picked his chair up and carried it next to mine, creating the Angel sandwich that I'm now in the middle of.

Slade seems annoyed to have to sit in such close proximity to me, but he doesn't move. For a moment I thought he might take his plate over to the breakfast bar just so he doesn't have to be near me, but for whatever reason, he's decided to stay where he is.

As if he's standing his ground and enduring my presence. As if moving away might give the others the idea that I had displaced him, that I had more right to be there than he did.

Maybe I'm overthinking this. He just seems so angry that I'm here. I have a knack for being acutely aware when I'm not wanted somewhere.

To add insult to injury, I'm left-handed and Slade is right-handed, so our forearms keep crashing into each other as we try to eat. He glares at me each time it happens, as if I'm doing it on purpose just to annoy him.

Despite his grumpiness, every time the hairs on his arm connect with my forearm, I feel a little zip of electricity between us, a little tingle that radiates up my arm and then feathers out into my body.

Maybe it's his hatred emanating from him and shocking my pores, but each time it happens, there's a little crackle, a brief connection. Maybe like a moth to a flame, I'm drawn to the thing that might ultimately kill me.

Slade made meat lasagne for dinner, and it's fantastic. Saucy and cheesy and perfect, the various layers all made by hand. The kitchen has been emitting mouth-watering aromas for a while now. I have had little to eat in the last twenty-four hours, so my bar is set extra low, but even if I wasn't starving, I'd savor this meal.

In addition to the meat lasagne, Slade made Brick a special vegan version of the dish, and the guys tease him about his fake cheese and his large side salad.

He smirks. "Want a bite?" he asks me, gesturing at his plate.

"Sorry, what?"

"Want a bite of my vegan lasagne? See what you're missing?"

"Sure," I grin. "I went through a vegan phase a while back, actually. There's some pretty decent stuff available these days. They just need to work on the cheese."

"Yeah, it's the one thing they don't seem to be able to nail. I might get Slade to try his hand at it, see what he can come up with."

Slade rolls his eyes. "Yeah, just how I want to be spending my time. Making even more vegan crap for you."

Brick carefully prepares a forkful of his meal and feeds it to me.

The flavors are fresh and savory and citrusy. "Oh wow! This is amazing!" I exclaim, and Brick smiles proudly, even though he didn't make the dish.

I glance at Slade. "This is almost better than the meat version. In fact, it might be my favorite!"

From the way he's beaming at me now, I may as well just have announced that Brick is my favorite.

Aidan clears his throat, interrupting the flow of conversation. "Don't forget what's happening later." He gazes at me intently, as if he's playing out what's going to happen later in his mind. "You're not off the hook, Angel. You owe me."

"For now, I'm going to enjoy my dinner and I'll worry about that later, thank you." I dismiss him with a flick of my wrist.

He narrows his eyes at me.

I don't think he liked that, being dismissed. I think he's used to doing the dismissing.

As I work my way through my lasagne, and wash it down with a can of sparkling water, the guys make chitchat about some business deals they're contemplating. I don't recognize any of the names or places they mention, and it feels almost like they're speaking in code, their own language.

Every time I get the sense they're using certain words in place of others, I file away the things they're saying. There seems to be some talk about gambling, maybe some bars or clubs, which would make sense given what Roman shared back at the salon. And lots of talk about moving kitchen equipment and supplies.

I sit and listen to them talk, more chatter about the incoming 'kitchen equipment'. I'm still not buying it. These four incredibly hot men are not making their money selling overhead vents and top-of-the-line stovetops to the restaurants around here.

I want to decipher their code to see just how criminal their activities really are, and what they're prepared to move through the islands to turn a profit.

Glancing around their opulent apartment, it's only logical that whatever they're involved in can't be legal. Nobody makes this much money unless they're involved in something shady. And innocent people don't have armed killers hunting them down in hair salons.

I'm thinking maybe they're involved with guns or drugs. Hopefully, it's not kidneys or humans or worse. I shiver as I think about the types of activities they might be involved in.

But what do I know? I'm not sure what their backstories are, or why they do the things they do. I'm not here to judge them for how they keep afloat in this uncertain world. It's not like I'm Ms. Morals doing everything the way society tells us to.

It's not like we all haven't found a way to get by, found a life that we can justify, even if others might judge it as morally gray. After all, we only have ourselves to answer to in the end.

I look around the table, letting my gaze rest for a moment on each of them. They're all so incredibly good-looking, and they're clearly very close, bantering back and forth as if they can read each other's minds.

It's confusing being here with them, sitting around the table as if I'm a special guest in their home rather than someone who's been kidnapped and brought here against my will. They treat me as one of them throughout the meal, passing me bread and salad and making sure I have enough lasagne. I'm a prisoner, but sitting here I feel for once like I belong, like I'm meant to be here.

Generally, I prefer to be by myself, a solo act. It's not often I get invited to spend time with others, and I've intentionally pushed everybody away to ensure that's the case. But there's an odd comfort in sitting with others at dinner and feeling like everyone accepts me having a seat at the table.

Well, everyone except Slade, who has glared at me the entire time and is continuing to do so right now. I can see him in my peripheral vision, sitting right beside me and scowling at me.

I want to call him out, but I'm scared that if I do, if I draw attention to myself, they might suddenly all decide they don't want me here and either lock me in my room or worse.

My mind flashes back to the last time I sat around a family table for a meal with my parents and my brother.

It must be the holidays, because otherwise my parents are rarely home at the same time. They're ships passing in the night with their multiple jobs and, in my dad's case, extracurricular activities.

We're sitting around the table that Mom has intricately decorated with festive napkin holders and candles and paper decorations. She always goes over the top, finding something new to add to the already busy decorations.

The center of the table is full of delicious holiday items. Carved, roasted turkey with cranberry sauce. Roasted Brussels sprouts. Herb stuffing. Mashed potatoes and gravy. Parker house rolls.

The aroma of each dish co-mingles into a cacophony of festive flavors, butter and roast turkey skin and garlic the most prominent tones.

The dining table is alive with the sounds of chatter and laughter, the clinking of silverware against ceramic plates, and the chewing noises of children trying to use their best table manners.

My mother looks tired, but she's smiling. I know the holidays are important to her, giving her a brief reprieve from the jobs that work her to the bone.

My father, taking a moment for once to spend time with his wife and children rather than taking on jobs he can't speak about that barely pay the bills, and chasing skirts all over the country under the guise he's 'traveling for work'.

It feels like we're in some Hallmark movie, frozen in time, where we're doing something families are meant to do, and actually enjoying it.

If anyone saw us here like this, they'd likely assume it was like this all the time. That my parents enjoyed each other's company, our company, and that our lives were light and fun and joyful. It's a lie, but one I'll happily take part in until it's over and things will go back to normal.

We're all laughing as my baby brother tells a story about school. He's so cute with his missing front tooth and a smattering of freckles across his nose.

I add to his joke, embellishing it to make it even more ridiculous. He giggles with joy, and everyone around the table laughs with us.

But then my brother looks directly at me, his eyes locking onto mine.

His lips thin and curl into a tight grimace as his pupils turn into tiny black pinpoints. His entire face changes, his cuteness fading as his flesh melts away to reveal a decomposing skull crawling with worms and other hungry insects.

Transformation complete, his rotting lips curve up in an evil smile and he bares tiny pointed teeth in my direction.

His mouth opens wider than it should, tilting back like a cap from a toothpaste tube, and he lets out a bloodcurdling scream.

Suddenly, there's blood everywhere, and my brother is covered in gaping stab wounds. He grins at me, his expression unhinged, and starts walking toward me with jagged, limping steps. As he advances on me, his flesh flays itself from his body, peeling away to reveal the muscles and tendons underneath.

My dead brother has almost caught up to me, his corpse disintegrating but still holding him together enough for him to keep limping toward me.

He wants to take me with him, to drag me into hell.

He cackles as he gets closer and pulls a scythe from behind his back, raising it above his head and preparing to slash it across my body. He wants me to be as disfigured and ruined as him.

I need to get out of here.

I hear screaming, and male voices saying, 'Angel, Angel.'

I tap my clavicle bone. Tap, tap, tap. Just the way my therapist showed me. Tap, tap, tap. You are safe. You are present. He can't hurt you. You are safe. You are present. He can't hurt you.

The screaming is me. The screaming is me. Stop screaming, Angel. He can't get you. Stop screaming.

I snap back to reality as a hand touches my shoulder.

For an instant I think about slapping it away, but the tapping worked, reminding me I'm not watching my brother as he's stabbed to death. That some sick, evil version of him doesn't exist, and he's not really after me.

He's gone, but it was a long time ago. I'm not here with him, and it was just another flashback trapped in a nightmare.

I glance around the table, eight eyes studying me with a combination of confusion and surprise. I'm here with my kidnappers who grabbed me because I witnessed one of them murder someone. Fuck. I'm glad my brother's decomposing corpse isn't about to annihilate me, but my current situation is hardly ideal, either. Talk about a rollercoaster of emotions.

There's not much worse than being in a nightmare, realizing you are, so you wake yourself up, feeling relief you're not in that nightmare anymore, but then quickly realizing your real life is worse.

A wave of grief washes over me, and I blink back tears as I think about how I lost everyone from my mind's dinner table scene at the hands of a complete psycho. And not just them, either. He went much further than that, working his way through everybody I cared about until there was nobody left who could give a flying fuck about Angel Benson. Although that wasn't my name back then. I will never speak that name again. She's dead.

He says he did it for me.

Intuitively, I know I can't blame myself, that his justification is just part of his psychopathy, but it's much easier said than done.

I'm the one he was after, that he's still after.

I'm his reason.

I can never get my family or friends back, and they live on only in my memory. I'm scared because some of my memories are already fading, and one day I fear that all I'll have is a couple of photos with no context.

I don't want the day to arrive when I don't remember the sound of my brother's innocent laugh or the way he would giggle when I'd pick him up for a hug. My parents were far from perfect, but I miss them, too.

I miss my good friends who were like rocks when going through all the things that life threw at us. The frantic text messages I sent to them, warning them, going unread since the night they died. Their Facebook profiles are deafeningly quiet, just an odd tribute post or memory from a relative or friend now and then.

Luckily, the crazed lunatic who killed them all is securely

locked up facing life in a maximum security prison thousands of miles from here, but I've always known it may not always stay that way.

So these guys I'm sitting with, breaking bread, might be bad guys.

They might do really fucked up things.

But if they do try anything crazy, there's a good chance they'll regret it.

Because what they don't know is that I have nothing left to lose.

And I'm a pro at saving myself.

"Angel, are you okay? You were just really out of it." Roman looks at me with concern.

"Did I fall asleep?"

"No, you just looked… like you were here, but you weren't inside anymore. And then you made this noise like you were trying to scream with your mouth closed."

"Ugh, sometimes I wake up from a nightmare doing that."

"You've done that before?" Aidan asks.

"Not while sitting at the dinner table. Maybe you gave me a severe concussion when you knocked me out twice in one day," I glare at Aidan and Roman. "I'm going to call you the Knockout Crew."

Aidan smirks. "We've been called worse."

"I gave you so much opportunity to spend the day fully conscious," says Roman, "but you just couldn't behave yourself."

"Yeah, you had a chance to be a good girl, Angel," says Aidan, his eyes on my lips. My pussy clenches when he uses those words, reminding me he's got a punishment to dish out to me later. "But you couldn't just do what Roman said at the salon. And then you tried to attack me in the car several times. You really brought everything on yourself. Well, everything after the murder. That wasn't your fault. You were just collateral damage."

"Okay, sure Aidan. You're the boss," I say, rolling my eyes.

He gives me a warning look, but then goes back to talking to the guys.

I take a deep breath, trying to push the flashback from my mind as I finish my lasagne.

My attention floats back to the conversation at the table, and once again I listen as the guys cryptically allude to business pursuits.

I look at each of them again.

Aidan and Slade seem like the more serious of the four, planning and anticipating different courses of action they might need to take, and assessing the risks involved. Aidan seems to approach things from a neutral perspective, while Slade seems to assume the worst in everything.

Brick and Roman seem more low-key, like they still very much care about the business but are more willing to go with the flow than needing to be the ones setting the direction. I also get the sense they might be the more impulsive ones in the group, that Aidan and Slade might need to pull them back from danger now and then. They seem to elaborate on Aidan and Slade's ideas with suggestions involving a lot of violence and risk-taking. Brick, in particular, seems to want everything to happen right now. Roman's sense of urgency seems to depend on what works with his calendar.

What the four clearly have in common is that they're all hot as fuck. I really don't mind being here, around this table with them. Whatever happens later on, I'll worry about it later. For now, I'm content watching and listening to them.

After a few minutes of conversation, I feel something brush against me, touching my knees. Trying not to react too obviously or draw attention to myself, I lean back slightly in my seat and try to get a look underneath the table, but I can't see what's happening from my current position.

I refocus on their conversation but then I feel it again, and this time whatever it is tries to press my knees apart. I squeeze them together and look around the table. That's when I see Aidan's eyes locked on me, his eyes twinkling and his mouth turned up in a smirk.

He nods at me, almost imperceptibly. Oh my god, it's his foot, and he's trying to wedge my legs apart. He bites his lower lip as he gazes at me and pushes his foot toward me again, wedging it between my knees.

I let his food spread my knees apart slightly, and he brushes his foot further up my inner thighs, causing them to tingle. He keeps moving his foot closer to my core until it rubs against my pussy through my shorts. I stare at him, my eyes growing large as I realize what he's doing.

He uses his foot to stroke me while he engages in conversation with the rest of the guys. My pussy throbs at his touch, little ripples emanating out from where his foot makes contact.

I know this is a test. He wants to see if I'll let on what's happening, if I'll let him continue doing what he's doing without saying anything.

The truth is, his foot feels fucking good rubbing against me while I sit here, and I don't want him to stop. My body has been on edge with everything happening, and Aidan is hot as hell. It's a turn-on that he's doing this while the other guys sit there, oblivious, scarfing down their lasagne while he manipulates my body.

Locking my eyes with his, I spread my thighs wider to give him more access. My pussy throbs intensely, and I feel myself getting increasingly wet as he flicks his foot up and down my slit through my pants. As he narrows in on my clit and rubs against it rhythmically, I feel my arousal dripping from me, soaking my panties.

I raise my gaze to meet his and bite my lower lip. I need his touch directly on my skin. My body is craving more of him. His fingers, his mouth, all of him.

My mind drifts to what my supposed punishment is going to be after dinner. Clearly, his foot is intended to be foreplay. My entire skin feels tingly, like it's lit up in anticipation of what's coming.

He flicks at my clit with his toe, grinding it against me, and I ball my hands into fists at my side, taking a deep breath to avoid crying out.

I resist the urge to reciprocate by grinding my hips against his foot to further increase the friction because everyone would see. I'm surprised they haven't noticed anything by now, and I'm really struggling to keep my breath slow and my face neutral.

He's zeroed in on my clit now, caressing it through my shorts and panties, increasing the pressure.

I'm getting close now, even through the layers of fabric. I can feel a white-hot coil tightening in my lower abdomen.

I press my lips into a thin line and take a deep breath, and they all glance at me.

"Are you okay?" Bricks asks, peering at me. "You have a funny look on your face and you're breathing funny."

"Uh—yes, fine. I'm fine," I say quickly, consciously slowing down my breath and forcing my face into a neutral position.

He shrugs. Everyone has finished eating, and he stands up to clear plates from the table.

Aidan removes his foot from between my legs and smirks at me as he stands up to help him.

My clit is aching, throbbing for more. I can't believe he stopped. I was getting really close. Then again, it would have been hard to not cry out at the dinner table and let on that Aidan was pleasuring me with his foot throughout our meal. I'm not sure what the other guys would think about that, although it's fairly safe to assume that Slade would not be impressed.

I leave dinner feeling very worked up, and hungry for my punishment.

As the other guys wash up, Aidan comes over and leans down behind me, his neck over my shoulder and his head parallel to mine. "Did you enjoy dinner?" he growls in my ear. A shiver of pleasure runs down my neck and makes my hairs stand on end as he tugs my earlobe gently with his teeth.

"Yeah, especially where some asshole reached out his leg and rubbed my pussy with his foot. That was unexpected," I hiss at him in a whisper.

"Are you complaining?" he asks, nipping me playfully on the curve of my neck.

"Not at all," I say, biting my lower lip. "It made dinner even more delicious. But I'd really like for you to finish what you started. I'm aching for you."

"Are you saying your cunt is aching for me, Angel? That you want me to bury my cock deep inside you? To rail you until your legs are like jello? You want me to make you fall apart over and over again until you can't remember your own name?" he growls.

I nod at him, my eyes pleading. I need him to give me a release.

"Which one?" he asks.

"All of them," I reply, my breath rapid as I picture him on me, in me, manipulating my body with his cock and his fingers and his tongue.

"Well, I'm glad you liked that, because I'm not sure how you're going to feel about what happens next. It's time for you to pay for how badly you've behaved today." He smacks me on my ass. "It's time to finally get what you've been asking for. Come with me."

CHAPTER 13

ANGEL

"Turn your ass around and face the table." Aidan looks truly annoyed, his eyes boring into mine and then trailing their way over my body. This time his gaze isn't just a general check-out, it's predatory. Like he's assessing which part of me he wants to eat first.

We're in an office with a large desk on one side of the room. It's located off to the side of the dining area where we just had dinner. I hadn't noticed this room before, and even if I had, I wouldn't have considered it a sex room.

Its walls are lined with wooden floor-to-ceiling shelves stuffed with books about business and economics, but also what appears to be an extensive fiction collection. They give this room that rich old book smell and I inhale deeply because it's one of my favorite scents in the world.

Okay, this room is more appealing than I realized at first glance. These guys are so hot they could make any room sexy. Books are sexy, and this space has lots of them. This room is blowing my mind.

As with the rest of the house, it's sleek and modern, with grand light fixtures and streamlined furniture. The desk is sturdy and metallic, the perfect height to be bent over and fucked against. But I'm not sure what he has in mind for me today.

I comply, placing my hands on the desk, and I hear the sound of him sliding the leather belt out of his belt loops. He cracks it loudly on the table next to me. I flinch at the startling sound and the vibration the belt creates on the table. I'm excited about what's coming, and a little shiver of anticipation runs through me.

He walks to the side, just out of view, and I turn to look at him over my shoulder.

"Don't you fucking turn around unless I tell you to," he growls. "You're really going to get it now."

My breath catches and I obediently follow his instructions, turning my neck back to neutral and focusing my eyes on the desk in front of me.

I hear him moving something, and then suddenly he's behind me again. I gasp as I feel cold metal pressing into the skin at the bottom of my shorts, skimming my butt and moving towards my inner thigh.

I shiver as the cool metal rises to the hem of my shorts, and instantly recognize the distinctive noise as he snips away at my clothing. He removes my shorts first, and then cuts off my panties, leaving my lower half completely bare. Too scared to look anywhere else but down, I see a flash of metal. I recognize what's in his hand. He's using my hairdressing shears to cut off my clothing.

"Where did you get those? They're my shears from the salon."

"Ro gave them to me as a souvenir of our special day."

I think better of telling him you're not meant to use them on anything but hair because it blunts the blades.

I shiver as he glides the sharp tip along my ass cheeks,

moving towards the center where he finds the cleft that marks the center of my butt.

"Bend over," he says, tracing the hairdressing shears down between my cheeks, letting them drag slightly against my very delicate flesh. He slowly slides the blade downward, keeping his pressure very light.

I gasp as the point of the shears skims over my back entrance. My breath grows faster as I wonder what's coming next, realizing his brother used the shears to kill someone in cold blood only hours ago.

These shears are extremely sharp, he's using them in a very sensitive area, and he's clearly unhinged just like the other guys in this house.

He continues to trail the points of the shears across my body, and just as he gets to my entrance, he pulls his hand away.

"No more unacceptable behavior or I won't stop there," he leans over and growls into my air, his breath hot against my earlobe.

He places the scissors over to the side of the room on the top of some drawers. I begin to straighten, as if to stand. "Did I tell you to move?" he growls.

I stay silent, my body tingling with goosebumps as I anticipate his next move.

"Answer me when I speak to you, brat," he snarls, and I jump.

Fuck. I keep making him madder, whatever I do. Probably not a good idea seeing he and everyone else in this house seems to be in a kill-y mood. Especially with my shears so close by. There's a fine line here between what might be fun and what might be deadly, and I don't know any of these guys well enough to tell the difference.

He presses me down with one firm hand on my upper back, and I feel the sensation of cold leather as he places the belt across my lower back, laying it flat on me and letting it sit there for a moment.

I shiver as I feel it lifting off me. There's a soft whoosh as leather cuts through the air before lashing the fullest part of my ass cheek with a loud thwack.

It stings like fuck and I try not to jump or cry out, but it's easier said than done and I feel myself flinch. My eyes water, but I squeeze them together as hard as I can and somehow hold in a gasp.

"You've been a very bad girl over the past twenty-four hours, Angel," he growls, "and this is what you get as your punishment. You need to learn what happens when your behavior is unacceptable."

I place more pressure on my forearms, flat on the table, and tense myself in anticipation of the next lashing.

He whips me again, harder this time. The area he made contact with stings and tingles, and I imagine the welts that are forming across my cheeks.

"Are you sorry for your behavior, brat?" he growls.

"Yes!" I cry out as he whips me again, no doubt adding another stripe to my cheeks.

"What are you sorry for?" he asks, revisiting the same spot as the first lash, the belt flogging me even harder than before. The smell of leather fills the air, and the sheer masculinity makes my pussy clench.

"Lying to Roman," I grimace as the belt thwacks against me again. My eyes are watering more now, but I'm determined for him not to see me cry.

"That's right. He told me all about that. And when you lie to one of us, you lie to all of us," he says. "You were a bad girl, not sharing important information with him." He pauses, and I flinch in anticipation, not being able to see what he's doing behind me. "What else do you have to apologize for, Angel?".

"Not following instructions." I brace for more impact, but it doesn't come. He steps back and I can feel his eyes on me.

"That's right. Good girl. You should see your gorgeous ass right now," he growls, his voice husky. "It's an artwork. I'm quite proud of it, actually. Flushed, with several areas of pretty, raised flesh. I enjoy putting my mark on you."

He runs a finger over one of the welts as if fascinated by it, admiring his handiwork. His touch adds to the heat that swarms the locations where he's lashed me, my skin tingling further at his touch.

"What else am I punishing you for, brat?"

He strikes me again, and I hold my ass as still and tense as possible as the belt cracks down on my flesh. It hits the very edge of my folds, causing a stinging situation to radiate into my core and generate a little ripple of pleasure. My arousal hangs thick in the air.

"Leaving my bedroom without your permission!" I grind out, reeling from the sting of the latest lash of the belt.

"That's right," he says. "I let you know when you can come and go from the bedroom. Do you understand me? I control you and your activities in and out of the bedroom."

He cracks the belt down on my cheek again, and I grit my teeth and squeeze my hands flat against the table in a mostly successful attempt not to cry out.

My ass stings like hell, the welts tingling as my body's response kicks in, rushing to heal the swollen skin. Even though it's painful, there's an intense throbbing between my thighs. He can probably see my arousal from his vantage point.

"Let me look at you," he says, taking a step back. He groans as he examines me. "It looks like you enjoyed your punishment. Your cunt is gushing."

I can't explain it. I need this type of pain.

I moan as he extends a long finger and slides it inside me. It glides in smoothly, through my arousal, with absolutely no resistance, and I buck against it. He growls and slides it out, wiping my juices on my ass.

He moves to the counter and I hear him pick up the shears again. I shiver as I wonder what he's going to do now, but this time it's a shiver of anticipation and desire. He might kill me at the end of this, but I'm enjoying the process.

A gasp leaves my lips as once again I feel the cold metal against my skin, but this time he gently presses it through my folds and collects some of my wet heat. Using his free hand, he grabs my arm to pull me up to standing and turn me around.

"Open your mouth and taste yourself, like a good girl," he growls, extending the shears toward my face.

I do what he says. I'm really hoping I still have a tongue after he's done with me. As I lick my juices off the shears, I maintain eye contact with him.

The same shears that took a man's life earlier.

Holy fuck. This is insane.

He gently twists the blade of the shears against my tongue and I feel a sharp prick, and then warm blood begins to flow gently into my mouth. He removes the shears and grabs me by the throat, pulling my mouth to his.

I tremble, my skin prickling as he swipes his tongue through my lips and explores my tongue with his, tasting a combination of my blood and my wet heat and sucking it into his mouth. He groans as he savors me. "Fuck, you taste so good, Angel."

I moan as he gently sucks on my tongue.

He suddenly yanks his head away and walks to the other side of the room.

"Get back into position, hands on the desk and bend over," he barks.

I do what he says, but I'm uncertain I can handle too many more lashes with the belt right now. My body is still stinging, on edge from earlier.

I brace myself for impact, but I hear him get down on his knees behind me.

His hot breath fans across my pussy and his hand part my slick folds from behind. I gasp as he tilts his face underneath me sucks my clit into his mouth, massaging it with his tongue before licking his way along my slit and to my entrance.

He laps at my soaking cunt, drinking in my arousal.

"Oh my god, your pussy is perfect. You taste so fucking sweet," he says, humming against me and sending vibrations throughout my cunt.

He swirls his tongue around my clit and then strokes it with one of his long fingers. He moves his tongue back down to my entrance and slides it into me, exploring my walls and coaxing more arousal from me, drinking it all in as he continues to massage my clit.

I grind my hips back against his face as he devours me. He cups my ass cheeks for leverage as he feasts on me, sliding his tongue in and out of my hole and over my folds, lapping at my clit, tasting every part of me he can access.

"Mmm, you're going to come for me now, baby, aren't you? I want you to come all over my face."

He spins himself around underneath me so that his front is facing mine and focuses his tongue solely on my clit. I feel two of his fingers sliding into my wetness until his knuckles are flush with my entrance.

His other hand holds me still so that all I can do is bend over and take it while his tongue lashes at me.

He fucks me with his fingers, spearing them into me as his tongue suctions onto my clit. I moan as he bites down gently and continues to unravel me stroke by stroke.

The room is quiet except for the sound as he works my wetness with his powerful hands. My eyes roll back in my head and my pussy clenches around his fingers, my hips bucking and writhing under his skilled touch as I start to get close.

"You're going to come for me soon, aren't you, baby? I can feel you getting close."

He slams his fingers inside me as far as they can go and sucks and slurps on my swollen clit as I buck and shudder against his hand and face, my body completely under his spell. An orgasm crashes through me and I see stars on the back of my eyelids as he continues to eat me while I squirm. I clamp my thighs together as firmly as I can around his face, and he groans and continues to lap at me while my whole body shudders with pleasure.

As my body stops twitching, he pulls his mouth away from my pussy, sliding his fingers out of me and standing up. I turn around to face him and he narrows his eyes as he stands there, both of us panting, his face slick with my arousal.

His eyes trail over me, dark with desire, and his cock stretches tight against his pants.

"Back in your room, Angel. Now!" He suddenly says, his voice raised, and points toward the stairs, dismissing me.

I look at him, questions in my eyes, but he just glares and continues to point.

I walk out of the office and toward the room, bottomless, my only shorts and panties snipped to pieces with my own shears. Glancing back over my shoulder, I see he's putting on his belt, his cock still straining against his pants.

I don't know quite what to make of what just happened. I'm surprised he didn't try to fuck me. His body clearly wanted to, maybe it's his mind that wasn't so sure for some reason.

But there are two things I know.

That I've never been as turned on in my entire life.

And that Aidan is a giant tease. And he's also a psycho. Just like his brother.

CHAPTER 14

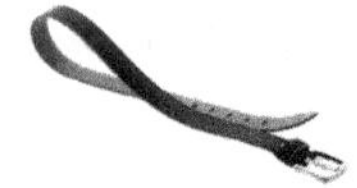

AIDAN

Fuck, that was hot. It's been a while since I've spanked a hot piece of ass. And it wasn't just any ass. It's certainly up there on my list of the nicest ones I've ever laid eyes on.

Angel was so sexy, the way she was clearly enjoying that pain as it melded with her pleasure. Her gorgeous rounded cheeks growing pinker and redder each time I brought the belt down hard on her creamy flesh. Marking her and making sure she'll feel me for days every time she sits down.

She's open-minded and sex-positive, I can tell. Two things that are really important if you want to succeed around here.

Besides her gorgeous tattoos, I noticed that her body was also covered in scars. Like, smothered in them. Some were raised like they were more recent or from a more serious injury, some little silver spidery lines that seemed to have been there for a while or are just more superficial. They vary in their angles and depths, making me think more than one tool or weapon was responsible for inflicting them.

I wonder how she got them, of course, but I didn't ask her

because I had other things on my mind. Like spanking her hot ass and plunging my tongue into her soaking cunt.

I'm still worked up from earlier and I get hard again thinking about all the things I want to do to her, and how sweet she tastes. I want to trace my fingers and my mouth along each scar, and learn the angles and little details of her body that I haven't yet had the chance to acquaint myself with.

By the time I was done with Angel's punishment, her ass was a palate of reds and pinks and creams, like I'd turned her into an even more beautiful creation than she already was. I didn't think it was possible. I should have taken a photo so I can relive our little encounter. Although maybe not having one gives me reason to do it all over again.

As I whipped her, I couldn't help but notice how her creamy thighs opened slightly for me, giving me a better view of her pussy, glistening with her arousal by the time I was done with my belt. I could smell her arousal in the air, and she was so sweet I couldn't resist having a taste. Seeing how wet she was, tasting her, it took everything I had not to come in my pants.

I could hear her breath quicken as I went, and she did a good job not crying out several times when I deliberately lashed her in the same spot to amplify the pain. She's definitely brave, even leaning into the agony of the belt. Trying so hard to hide the fact it hurt, even though I could see the aftermath on her body.

Her skin was flushed and covered in a slight sheen by the time I was done, emanating heat. She was so fucking hot, she had me as hard as an iron bar.

The way she took the lashing, it's like spanking her with my belt gave her life, like it filled a void deep inside of her, just for that moment. It's almost like she was craving, desperate for this kind of release.

She was soaking wet by the time I was done whipping her, and I'm going to jerk off to memories of the sounds her pussy made as I finger fucked her, and the way her arousal released onto my hands and my face.

I could have fucked her if I'd wanted to. I know she wanted my cock buried inside her sweet cunt. But I'm going to make her wait a moment.

She doesn't need to know I had to come straight to my room to relieve myself. That I'm picturing her curvy ass and the way her cunt dripped for me, pleading for my cock. But I will not give it to her that easily.

I want her to crave it.

I want her to beg for me.

And soon she'll be screaming my name.

CHAPTER 15

ANGEL

A while after I retreat to my room, the door opens and Brick comes strolling in. He stands just inside the entrance, clearly inside 'my' space, and turns to me.

Maybe he feels like he has carte blanche to come in whenever he wants now because he freed me from his torture basement. But there's no announcement, no knocking on the door to see if I'm decent. He just walks in like he owns the place, which technically, I suppose, he does along with the other guys.

It's fine, though. I've just been sitting on the bed bored out of my brain so I don't mind the interruption, if you can even call it that. My back is propped against the pillow with my head tilted back, because there's literally nothing to do except stare at the ceiling. I turn my head to look at him.

His gaze travels over my body and lingers on my bare lower area and I feel myself flush.

"Jesus, he didn't waste any time getting to know you, did he?" he chuckles. "That's our Aidan, although it's more of a Roman move, if I'm honest."

There's a burning sensation in my stomach at the thought of

Aidan doing what he just did to me, to anyone else. It felt special between us, not something that he does regularly with new women he meets. But it's probably naïve of me to think that way. We just met, and who knows how he operates? Slade says I'm nothing special, and maybe Aidan thinks that, too.

Aidan is interesting. He's clearly so used to leading the group, so dominant, and it definitely extends into the bedroom with him. He's fixated on making people submit to him.

I've barely met the guy, and he's already comfortable whipping me with his leather belt, marking me with welts. And then what he did with my hairdressing shears. And his fingers and his tongue. Just remembering it is enough to send a shiver of pleasure shooting through me.

I'm never going to be able to work, to hold the shears in my hand, without thinking about what he did with them. My clients are all going to wonder why I'm blushing and have hard nipples while I'm giving them a shag cut with curtain bangs.

I grab a pillow from the head of the bed and modestly place it over my pussy because Brick is still staring at it.

"Oh, you're shy now, are you?"

"Not shy," I shrug. "Just wasn't expecting you to wander in here while my pussy's out."

"I'm not complaining. Totally fine about seeing your pussy, clothed or unclothed. I don't believe you've formally introduced us, though. Just give me the word and I'd be happy to say hello."

I smirk. "She's shy. And she's had enough visitors for the day. Needs time to recharge."

Brick laughs. "Fair enough. Speaking of which," he extends his hand to me, "here, these are for you."

I cautiously take what appears to be a ball of bunched-up black fabric.

Unfurling it, I see it's a pair of familiar-looking underwear.

"Hey, these are mine! Where did you get these?"

"We got some of your stuff from your apartment so that

you'd be comfortable," he explains. "I'll bring the rest up later. These were just, uh, for safekeeping."

"You *stole* my underwear from my apartment?"

"More like borrowed," he shrugs. "See, I'm returning them now. It's a bit like a library, you see. Took them for a spin."

"You'd better not have jerked off on these," I say, narrowing my eyes as I inspect them.

"Oh, I didn't jerk off *on* them," he grins. Jesus.

All of them are unhinged.

Roman, Aidan and Brick most certainly are.

I haven't interacted much with the one who was cooking earlier except to know he strongly dislikes me.

But if three out of four are complete psychopaths, then chances are good the fourth one is as well.

CHAPTER 16

ANGEL

I t's the morning, and I slept surprisingly okay for someone who's been kidnapped by a bunch of hot psychopaths. The bed was comfortable, and I'm sure my body and mind desperately needed to recharge after everything that's happened over the last couple of days.

Brick did as he promised last night and dropped off a bunch of my stuff, all shoved haphazardly into a duffel bag, and left it outside the door to my room.

I tip the contents of the bag onto the bed. There are tank tops and shorts and T-shirts and dresses and leggings. Underwear and some toiletries.

Brick did a good job throwing this together in a rush, especially considering the state I left my apartment in. What can I say? I keep my salon immaculately clean, but the same can't be said about the space where I live. It's just not a priority and I've never been that good at cleaning or organizing my own stuff. You win some, you lose some.

I pore through the items and pick out a clean outfit. Fresh panties and a sports bra, shorts and a racer-back shirt. Dressing for the island weather. I'll no doubt look more casual than The Brothers Fancypants downstairs, but this casual beach style works for me.

Hopping into the shower, I let the hot water run over me, cleansing me from the craziness of the past forty-eight or so hours and my interaction with Aidan that left arousal dripping down my thighs. The guys were thoughtful, remembering makeup and hair products, and I emerge from my bedroom looking relatively well put together in the circumstances. I tie my hair into a topknot and secure it with a bandana.

There's a knock on my door. "Angel, can I come in?"

It's Roman.

"Yep! I'm decent," I call out.

"That's no fun! I don't want to come in then," he jokes, as he opens the door.

He's so fucking handsome, and he's also had a shower and changed by the looks of it. He's wearing a fitted polo shirt that shows off his muscular body, and dress shorts. It's a step more casual than I've seen him so far, but still very smart, like he could attend a business meeting in this outfit and nobody would blink an eye. I'm sure all of his clothing is designer, and that a tailor was involved in getting everything to fit the way it does.

He smells great, too. His cologne today is a refreshing, masculine scent I want to say is a pleasing combo of yuzu, sage and cardamom.

"You look cute," he says, appraising me. "I like your shorts."

"Oh yeah? They're just shorts."

"That's an understatement. I like them because they're so short that you don't even have to bend over and I can see the curve of your gorgeous ass. It's sexy as hell, and I'm going to be staring at your butt for the rest of the day."

I grin mischievously. "Slade will be mad if he sees me distracting you with my ass."

Roman laughs. "I'm sure he'll get over it when he sees why

I'm distracted. He may not like to fuck anymore, but he can appreciate the beauty of the female form."

I grin. I don't mind these compliments one little bit. Especially from a man as gorgeous as Roman.

"Anyway, I've officially come here to collect you. You've earned some time out of your room because of your good behavior. We'd like to reward you with some chill-out time. The downside is you have to spend time with all four of us, not just me."

Oh my god, yes. Finally. I can get out of this room and do something more interesting than just wait and stare at the ceiling. I can get out of my own thoughts. Also, I want more time around these guys to see what makes them tick. I haven't quite untangled their interpersonal dynamics.

On the face of it, I think Brick would probably be the easiest to manipulate, or maybe Roman.

Brick is a bit like a puppy dog around me, his eyes growing big whenever he sees me. An underwear-stealing puppy. If he had a tail, it would wag like crazy as he tried to come up with more and more ways to impress me.

Roman is clearly used to manipulating women to get pussy. I don't think he's used to his wiles being turned around on him and that makes him vulnerable.

Slade and Aidan will be harder nuts to crack.

They're both on the lookout for any hint of risk, and even though Aidan doesn't seem to automatically assume the worst like Slade does, both seem highly attuned to someone trying to pull one over on them.

This is all speculation at this point. I don't have a ton of data points and a lot is based on my gut and my understanding of human motivations. I need more information, and to know all of them better so I can figure out the best way to take them down so I can escape.

"Really? You're saying I get to… not be locked in a room? That's so exciting!" I clap my hands together. "Don't tease me with bodily autonomy. I might get used to it."

He smirks. "It's just for a little while, Angel. Think of it as a test. If you don't fuck up too bad, and if you're a good girl, you might get to do it again."

The way he says good girl, his voice a husky growl, does things to me. My pussy clenches hard. I'm going to have dreams about him calling me that while he buries his cock deep inside me. I hold in a moan as I think about Aidan saying the same thing yesterday when he gave me my punishment.

"I promise to be a good girl this time," I wink, and his eyes darken with lust, the words clearly affecting him, too.

He clears his throat and speaks quickly, as if slowing down might make him change his mind, as if instead of taking me to hang out with the other guys, he might throw me onto the bed and bury himself inside me. "We have to go downstairs right now. The others are expecting you and they'll get pissed if we don't come down soon."

He pauses. "And if you keep talking dirty to me, I'm going to lock myself in here with you instead and spend the entire night fucking you until I break your pussy. So let's get the fuck out of here before there's no going back."

He grabs me by my wrist and pulls me out of the room, shutting the door behind us, part of me wanting to yank him back in there and spend hours doing all the things he just mentioned.

We head to the living room to join the other guys, my pussy throbbing, and I take a seat in the middle of the sectional couch, next to Aidan. Roman squeezes in next to me on my other side. Slade sits on the furthest end, on the other side of Aidan.

Brick is perched on the arm of an armchair across from us because there's no way we could all fit on the couch at once. They're all so big and tall and muscular, and it makes me feel tiny being sandwiched between them. They might be scary guys, but I kind of like this feeling, like any of them could crush me with one hand. It might be playing with fire, thinking that way, but I like what I like.

On my way to the living room, I got more of a sense of just

how huge this place is. The living room alone is many times the size of my shithole of an apartment, with high ceilings and a couch that could probably fit six to eight regular people, but only three of these guys and me. They're just all so big.

The entertainment system is state-of-the-art, with a massive screen with surround sound and a variety of remote controls that probably take a PhD to figure out how to operate. Thank goodness for voice-controlled technology.

They talk amongst themselves about an upcoming delivery. On the surface, it's about some type of kitchen equipment, but once again I get the feeling they're speaking in code. Whatever it is, it's clear that something's coming to the island that's most likely very illegal, and they're making plans to receive it and transport it onward to the next location.

I try to act like I'm not listening, that I'm focusing on the TV that plays quietly in the background. I even pretend to doze off now and then. That has to be believable after they knocked me out twice in one day. There have to be some residual side effects of being smacked unconscious, hopefully not permanent ones.

I figure I may as well try to get as much information as I can just by listening to these guys. Once they're more comfortable with me around, I might even casually ask a few questions. It might be the only way I can get out of here. Information might be as useful as having a key to the lock on my bedroom door.

At least I know I'm good at escaping.

I've run from scarier than this.

I look around the room at each of the guys.

Aidan carries himself and speaks like he's the clear leader of their group. He seems serious, thoughtful, intentional and methodical. Responsible, reliable, and consistent. All of these dad-like adjectives, but he looks nothing like my dad. He's fucking sexy. Close-cropped dark hair that he often runs his hand through when he's thinking. Piercing hazel eyes that simmer when he makes eye contact with me.

Plush lips, his lower one slightly moreso, that I just want to tug at with my teeth. That he used to rub against my folds while he was feasting on my pussy.

The gentle throbbing continues between my legs at the memory of how skilled he is with his tongue and his fingers. And what he did with my shears that I'll never look at the same way again. He's given me a hairdressing shears fetish. My heart flutters and my pussy clenches hard, and I want nothing more than to feel him dragging the cold metal against the most sensitive parts of my body, breaking my flesh and tasting my blood.

The others seem to defer to Aidan, waiting for him to make decisions and answer questions that are anything more than straightforward. Like he's always the one who knows what to do.

I imagine that must get overwhelming at times, having other grown men relying on you when you're probably just trying to figure things out like everyone else.

I'll file that away, and see if it comes in useful later on. Maybe I can drive a wedge between the guys and make a run from it while they work through the conflict.

While Aidan's calm, he's not devoid of human emotion. He was clearly pissed at me before, after I attacked him in the car, but he seems to have calmed down since he took his feelings and emotions out on me with his belt.

A shiver runs through me, but it's not unpleasant. The thwack of the leather still feels very close to my body, my ass is still a little tingly and some of the red marks are still very visible.

I got a little thrill earlier when I saw them in the mirror after my shower. I wish I had my phone so I could take a picture and remember the way he marked me forever. So I could send it to him as a reminder if he was having a bad day, or if I wanted to jump his bones the moment he got home from a job. But I'm getting ahead of myself. It's not like I'm going to be here forever.

He was just so sexy with the belt, so in control, making me ride the fine, fine line between pleasure and pain. He knew exactly how to mark me like I was his pretty picture, and how to make me feel something, anything, for the first time in a very long time.

He was sexy. It was raw. It was just what I like.

Because I like a little punishment now and then. I like to feel.

Brick is quite different from Aidan. He seems to be the enforcer for the group.

He's brutish and clearly very strong, not opposed to a little torture.

I've noticed that except for the first time I saw him in the basement, he seems to always be wearing a leather jacket. It seems to be his signature look, even though I've only seen him a few times.

He seems quirky, but caring, like when he didn't want me to have to stay on the piss- and shit-stained, grimy mattress in his torture chamber, shackled to his wall. How he insisted on begging for forgiveness rather than asking for permission when he snuck me out of his torture basement and into a spacious, clean spare bedroom.

Despite his obvious quirks, his basement is incredibly well-organized. I don't know if he forces himself to be that way because it's his pride and joy, or whether it comes naturally to him when it comes to his work.

Based on something primal I can sense about him, besides just being an incredibly large and strong human being, I imagine he's into some filthy, nasty sex, but that's a hunch I still need to verify.

I haven't figured out Slade yet. He's quiet, brooding. He spends a lot of his time in the kitchen, and it seems to be by choice. It's like he wants to be around the group, but from a distance.

He's part of the pack but tends to physically position himself away from it, listening, and thinking, quietly observing.

I almost smack myself in the side of the head as a light bulb goes off. Slade is a fucking cat. In human form.

And like a housecat that doesn't like visitors, by the way he's been scowling and glaring at me ever since I arrived at this house, it's not hard to figure out he doesn't want me here.

Well, the feeling's mutual, buddy. I don't want to be here, either.

And then Roman, of course, is a big flirt. He's good at it, too. A true player, a master fuck boy. Charming and charismatic, able to boost your confidence to the highest high so that your inhibitions and your panties disappear.

Maybe there's more to him, but that's all he's shown me so far.

Well, and that he's a violent murderer who will knock me out without a second thought.

I shiver, goosebumps forming on my arms. He could have killed me at the salon too, and it would have been easier for them to clean up than having me here at their house.

I wonder what stopped him, and then what stopped the larger group, because they don't seem like nice guys that would dish out a softer punishment just because I'm a woman.

I have a feeling they're all pretty ruthless, and that they'll do what they need to do to come out on top.

The scope of their business dealings seems broad. From what Roman shared at the salon and what I've been able to piece together while here, they have a diverse set of interests here on the island. And some people in those industries don't fuck around—bars, clubs, strip clubs, underground gambling dens. Not one of those businesses is for the fainthearted.

And if the kitchen supply warehouse really is a front for trafficking guns and drugs and god knows what else, they have to be pretty hard guys themselves.

Clearly, not one of them is originally from this island. As usual, all four of them are well-dressed, not in the casual clothing that most guys wear around here. Roman's outfit from the salon yesterday seems to be par for the course. Nobody dresses like this here, the only uniforms being at hotels and fast food places. Their style makes no sense in this tropical climate. They stick out like sore thumbs, transplants from the mainland just like me, although I do a better job of trying to fit in.

Instead of tank tops and board shorts, they wear tailored suits, and designer T-shirts and polos. The most casual their pants get seem to be jeans and dress shorts. This place is air-conditioned perfectly, so I'm sure they feel just fine in here. But when they exit into the island's thick humidity, I can't imagine they could be comfortable.

Instead of colorful flip-flops, they wear monochrome leather shoes that look like they must have cost a fortune. Brick is the exception with his retro sneakers. I'm a bit of a sneakerhead myself, so I appreciate his style. He generally looks one step more casual than the others with his tight-fitting polo shirt which wraps around his impressive torso, showing off his bulging pecs and biceps, and today he's wearing shorts that reveal muscular, tattooed calves.

They might be bad boys, and their style might be fussier than I've gotten accustomed to living in a tropical paradise, but they are also all hot as hell. At least I have four hot men to look at while I'm here.

I just have to hope that they don't kill me.

Or on second thought, maybe that would give me some peace at last.

I could finally stop running and looking over my shoulder. Of waiting for the rug to get pulled out and finding my way backsliding into terror when *he* finds me.

Not that I'm planning on telling these guys about any of that. About *him*.

After talking business for a while and figuring out that Brick and Slade will be the ones who will actually go pick up the ship-ment, they seem to remember I'm here and they all turn to face me. None of them says a word, but their eyes track over my body like they're seeing me for the first time.

"Um, hi?" My voice squeaks.

Aidan smirks. "Sorry, were we ignoring you, princess? Apologies for the lack of hospitality. Are you having fun yet?"

"Yes, so much fun," I roll my eyes. "Trapped here with the four of you. You're lucky you're all good-looking or I'd be trying harder to get out of here."

I may as well make this time as entertaining as possible. That way, they might not keep me locked in my room while they plot my death. I wouldn't mind another round of punishment with Aidan, and I'd like to get to know the others better as well.

"Oh really?" Roman looks at me and narrows his eyes. "You think all of us are good-looking?"

I nod. "Sure do. All four of you are hot as fuck. I thought it was a dream when I first saw you all together."

They glance at each other. I can't tell if they're amused or what, but they seem to be non-verbally communicating, and then all eight eyes turn back to me.

"I thought I was your favorite, seeing I'm the one that found you," Roman pouts.

"The jury's out," I say. "I don't know any of you yet, really. All I know about you, Roman, is that your hair smells nice, that you murder people and leave big puddles of blood all over the floor, and that you knock women out stone cold in their workplaces if they dare to stick up for themselves and try to escape while you're trying to kidnap them."

"That was a first for me, too," he says, putting his hands up in defense. "It's not my fault you're good at your job, and that's how I ended up at your salon. And I hardly knew that lunatic was going to run in there and point a gun at me."

I smirk, secretly pleased his extensive hair salon research led him to me. Even though this whole situation on the back end is less than ideal, it still feels nice to know I'm good at something and even a picky motherfucker like Roman is willing to give me a shot.

"So, do I get a house tour?" I ask the group, peering at them through my eyelashes. May as well try to act cute and see who seems most vulnerable to it. "You brought me here while I was unconscious and I've only seen a few rooms. The basement and the kitchen and dining area. This living room and…" I feel myself blushing and I glance at Aidan, "the office."

Aidan smirks and winks at me. "I've given you a deep dive tour in there."

I flush as I remember his tongue delving into my folds and piercing my entrance. Talk about a deep dive.

I realize I'm being held prisoner, but I figure if I act as confident as possible, as if I belong here, maybe they'll let me have a little more leeway while I figure out how to escape. Knowing the layout of the house might give me some ideas and some options.

"What do you think this is? An open home?" Slade narrows his eyes at me. "Would you like me to bake some cookies and leave them out on the counter for your tour?"

"Yeah, that sounds lovely. Could you avoid baking your salty personality into them, though, please?" I smile sweetly at him with the fakest smile I can muster.

His eyes narrow further, but Brick laughs. "She's got you all figured out already, bro."

Relief washes over me as Slade transfers his glare from me to Brick.

"Sure, we can take you on a tour," says Brick, grinning. "It sounds like fun."

Roman glares at him. "I'll come, too," he says.

"I'll keep an eye on you both," says Aidan.

"For fuck's sake, let's make it a family trip." Slade rolls his eyes. "I'll make sure none of you does anything stupid."

I don't know what his deal is, and I need to watch out for him.

———

They take me through the apartment to show me the many

rooms I haven't seen yet, all four guys and me padding around the giant compound.

Brick decides to play host, putting on a funny voice and announcing each room as we pass by.

"This is the powder room, where Aidan powders his nose," Brick makes flamboyant hand gestures at each doorframe as he gives us the rundown. "And here's the nursery where Roman wears duck-print onesies."

"Shut the fuck up, Brick," Roman and Aidan say in unison.

I laugh and Slade snorts but then stops himself when he glances over at me and sees me laughing, too.

I guess he hates me so much we're not allowed to find the same things funny.

I shiver under his icy gaze.

The property is expansive, with a bunch of extra spare bedrooms in addition to mine.

There's a game room with a pool table and shuffleboard, as well as every video game console you could think of. Vintage pinball machines and arcade games line one side of the room, and there's a fully stocked bar on the other side.

"You've seen my torture basement," says Brick, proudly gesturing down the stairs as we walk by. I shiver again, remembering the cupboard full of sinister equipment.

He points out a high-tech gym with a bunch of free weights and machines and cardio equipment, and large screens attached to the walls. No wonder they're all so fucking built. They have a state-of-the-art fitness center right in their home.

"What else is there to show you? I won't show you Roman's bedroom," says Brick, his eyes glimmering. "You can be the one woman on the island who hasn't seen it."

"I'm not that bad, Brick. Jesus!" Roman looks pissed, like I haven't picked up on the fact he's clearly a fuck boy.

"I thought you were a virgin when we met," I say to Roman. "I figured you'd have major problems getting laid."

Roman smirks. "Clearly, you need glasses."

I snort. "Humility's a noble trait. You should look it up."

"I'm not familiar," says Roman, winking at me.

"We won't show you the office, because you've already experienced that," Aidan taps my ass as he walks past me. My face flushes as I'm once again reminded of his tongue and his belt and my shears. All of it.

The throbbing continues in my core. The perpetual throbbing I've experienced in this house is driving me insane. Being around four drop-dead gorgeous men, as scary as they may be, it's like every look, every word they say in their sexy voices, every time they stretch or move near me, triggers more intense throbbing. And it's only getting worse. I desperately need a release before I explode into a puddle on the floor.

We make our way back to the living room, and everyone remains standing.

"And that," Brick gestures theatrically, "concludes our grand tour!"

"I have an idea," I say, suddenly. I'm worried if I don't speak up they'll just lock me in my room again. "Let's make a bet." I haven't thought this through at all, but I need to keep their attention away from me being a captive who should be shut away again.

"On what?" Brick raises an eyebrow.

"On who wins a contest."

"Pretty sure we can smoke you at just about any contest," snorts Slade.

"What kind of contest are you thinking?" Aidan asks, peering at me.

I think about it and then smile as an idea comes to me. "A hot dog eating contest."

The guys glance at each other.

"Well, this is going to be easy. It's your funeral," says Slade. "Have you seen how much food Brick can pack away? All of us, really, compared to you. Look at how much bigger we are!"

"And what do you want if you win?" Aidan raises an

eyebrow. "You must have something in mind. I don't think you woke up this morning and said 'hey, know what I want to do today? Stick all the hot dogs in my mouth and take them down as quickly as I can'."

"Imagine if that's what she really thought about when she woke up, though," grins Brick mischievously. "I would have lent her mine as practice."

"I don't want you to lock me in the bedroom anymore," I shrug, changing the subject back to what I want to win as a prize. The reason I came up with this random challenge in the first place. Freedom. "I want to be free to roam around the house whenever I want."

"What would stop you from escaping out the front door, never to be seen again? What if you stab us in our sleep?" Slade narrows his eyes at me.

"Both are tempting." I narrow my eyes back at him. "But in case you don't remember, you took my phone and all my belongings. We appear to be in some type of industrial area, and our closest neighbors are probably miles away, judging from the little I've seen."

"Okay, that covers off an immediate escape plan, kind of," says Aidan. "I'm still skeptical, though. What about the stabbing in our sleep part?"

"I guess that's just a risk you'll have to take. I am good with a pair of shears… just like you are, Aidan."

His eyes flick to mine and he bites his bottom lip, no doubt also remembering our time together in the office and what he did with my shears.

My tongue tingles as I remember him piercing it so that it bled, of him sucking my bloody tongue as if it were my clit. My pussy clenches hard. I want a round two. I want him buried inside me this time.

"Okay," he says, looking around at the group and then back at me. "If you win the bet, you can have privileges for twenty-four hours. Not forever."

"I guess that's a start, better than nothing," I shrug. "But, if I'm good for twenty-four hours, will you reconsider?"

"Maybe," he says, "if you're a good girl, anything is possible. But there's a very high bar."

Slade shakes his head and sighs. "This is yet another terrible idea."

"And what do you get if you win?" I raise an eyebrow and look at each of them. "Not that it's going to happen, but we should set the wager up front, so we're all clear about what's at stake."

They glance at each other without speaking, and the weirdest thing happens. After several exchanges of eye contact, they nod at each other as if they just had a detailed conversation out loud.

"We each get an hour with you, naked, to do whatever we want with you," says Roman, biting his bottom lip, "and I get to go first."

The other guys nod. I'm uncertain that they'd agreed to the Roman going first part in their silent conversation. He probably added that on in the moment, but they seem totally down with the naked hour idea.

I feel a deep twinge between my legs and the throbbing intensifies. Not that I'd let on, but Roman's idea of a prize for the guys seems like a reward for me, too. They're all so fucking hot.

The thought of spending an hour with each of them, getting to know their bodies and the way they like to be touched, and the way they like to touch me, makes my pulse race and my body heat. I'm tempted to let them win, but as much as I want to explore their gorgeous bodies, I want my freedom more.

"Good enough. Let's do it," I grin at the guys and, as usual, they all look at Aidan for the final decision.

Aidan nods. "Alright then, the bet is on. Let's go!"

We enter the kitchen, and Slade gets things ready. He lines up a row of hot dog buns and expertly slices each of them down the middle, placing a hot dog in each.

"Ketchup, mustard and relish or no?" He raises an eyebrow and glances at each of us.

"Nope! We have to do this by the book, guys," I say. "Official rules prohibit the use of condiments. It's considered cheating."

"What the fuck is by the book with a hot dog contest?" scoffs Slade. "The whole thing sounds juvenile, like something you'd do at a kid's party."

"It's a whole industry, Slade. People do this for a career. You can make a lot of money in the hot dog-guzzling biz." I shrug. "Don't ask me how I know this, but you have to eat the whole thing—bun and hot dog—to count. No utensils, no condiments. You can have water or any other liquid. You can only dip your hot dog and bun into your beverage for up to five seconds at a time."

"Sounds like an average Friday night for Brick," Roman cracks up laughing, and I snort. Brick's so weird I can picture him dipping his dick into random cups of soda while he watches vegan documentaries on the big screen.

Brick narrows his eyes at Roman. "Are you trying to say I don't last long, *player*?"

Aidan shakes his head and laughs as well. Slade rolls his eyes.

"Okay, now that we're done talking about Brick's sexual prowess and proclivities, are we ready for this contest?"

"Yep, I'm ready," says Brick. "My beverage of choice is whiskey!"

"Are you sure?" I raise an eyebrow. "I don't think that's a good idea. It's meant to help you get the bun down, not to get you drunk."

He grins. "It sounds way more fun my way."

"Okay, whatever you say," I shrug. It's his funeral.

While Brick prepares himself a generous pour of whiskey, the rest of us equip ourselves with glasses of water.

Aidan sets up a timer on his phone. "Alright, whoever eats the most hot dogs in five minutes is the winner!"

We all nod, poised over our respective plates.

"Three, two, one, and... go!"

Out of the corner of my eye, I see Slade ripping his hot dog in half before devouring each. He's a fast eater, practically inhaling the meat and bun.

Next to him, I see Aidan grab the protein first, swallowing it down in big bites. He dunks the bun in water and then chews quickly, rocking his body back and forth slightly to ease the contents down.

Roman rolls his bun into a small ball and takes large bites to get it down.

Brick dunks his hot dog in whiskey and bites off a giant chunk, slamming it into his mouth. "Fuck yeah, drunk dogs!" he yells with his mouth full of food. I want to laugh, but that takes time, so I choke it back and keep going.

My style is like Aidan's, but more advanced. I grab my hot dog and snap it in half. Each time I take a bite, I dunk the bun in water, take another bite, and then do it all over again. I'm methodical, laser-focused, and I need to win.

Everyone is so engrossed in what they're doing. The kitchen is silent except for the sounds of chewing and sipping and slurping, everyone deeply focused on shoving bits of meat and bread into their mouths and choking them down.

Slade reaches for a second dog, and Brick tries to hold his hand back. Aidan's on to his second as well. Brick is taking sips of whiskey in between bites which slows him down, pieces of hot dog bun becoming tangled in his beard.

Suddenly, the timer goes off and everyone stops mid-chew. We look around. Brick has half a hot dog sticking out of his mouth, and everyone else holds a fraction of a bun in their hand.

Looking at each of our stashes in front of us, mine is the most depleted.

"Holy shit, Angel. You ate five hot dogs?"

"Well, four-and-three-quarters if you want to get technical," I say, holding up my remaining fragment of bun, the tip of the hot dog poking out the end.

I glance at the counter in front of the others.

"Two and a half for me, but if you count the whiskey, I think I win!" exclaims Brick. "It was like a whiskey pairing, meaning I needed to take it slower to savor all the delicious tastes."

I snort and count the hot dogs on the other plates.

The others ate four each. Which means…

"And the winner is… Angel!" Brick holds my hand up high in the air like I just won a boxing match. "Weighing in way less than any of us, Angel has smoked the competition, stuffing her mouth with hot dogs and guzzling them down her throat in an attempt to avoid having each of us stuff her with ours!"

Slade glares at me, but there's a hint of something in his eyes, like he's a tiny bit impressed by my hot dog-eating skills.

"Twenty-four hours," says Aidan, glancing at his watch. "Starting… now."

"Yeah, make the most of it," says Slade, his eyes narrowing. "While you can."

CHAPTER 17

SLADE

Picking up our latest delivery gives me some alone time with Brick, which is good because I need to get him on side. This whole situation with Angel is getting out of control.

As he drives us toward the pickup spot, he glances over at me a few times, as if he knows I have something to say. But he, like the other guys, knows I'll talk when I'm ready. I like that they don't try to force me, to pry the words out when they're not fully formed. I prefer to think things through and make sure I'm precise before I start blabbering like other people do.

"I don't like her being at our house," I say, frowning.

"Angel? You've made that pretty clear," nods Brick, glancing over at me, and then he grins. "She's pretty, though. Nice to look at."

"Yeah, that's an understatement," I sigh. "It's part of the problem. The three of you are all running around at half-mast in her presence, not thinking about work. All obsessed with shoving your dicks into her. I'm worried she's a massive distraction, and she's going to come between us and our business."

There's no way I'm telling Brick that even though my dick hasn't worked quite right for years, even though sex is usually the last thing on my mind, she's caught my attention.

It twinges at the sight of her when she bends over to put something in the dishwasher, or when I get a glimpse of her nipples hard under her thin tank top. It twitches now just at the thought of seeing her in those vulnerable moments, when her body speaks to me and mine responds.

Nobody has made my body respond like this in a really long time, and it's got me on high alert. If she's got me like this, no wonder the other guys are sniffing around like crazy, unable to focus on the work at hand.

"We don't have to keep her around forever," shrugs Brick, as he turns down a side street towards where the drop point for our most recent imports. "But I'd really like to have some fun with her before we decide how we're going to dispose of her."

I sigh. "We're going to end up regretting this, man. I don't care how round her ass is or how good she probably is at sucking dick."

Brick laughs. "Hey, she might be a bit of a firecracker, but how much harm could she do? She's tiny compared to us, and there's only one of her." He shrugs. "And do you really think she's that big of a distraction? It's not like Roman isn't constantly distracted by pussy, anyway. Maybe it's better to have one for him to obsess over in the house rather than having him go out chasing it all over town. Gives him something to focus on at home. At least we know where he is at all times, stalking Angel around and trying to get into her pants."

I snort. He brings up a good point. "Fair. Although I can't say the same for you and Aidan. You like women and all, but you're usually not this distracted."

I glance at the GPS. "We're two miles away. Can you go a bit faster? I want to make sure nobody gets there first. I know the snakes aren't actively trying to stop us anymore, but that seems to have emboldened Zero and his guys."

Brick steps on the accelerator, and within a couple of minutes we're outside a warehouse that's dark except for a grimy exterior light pointed at a side door.

"Stay here," he says, unbuckling his seatbelt. It always amuses me that Brick is so set on wearing his seatbelt. This big guy who enjoys torturing and murdering people, who doesn't mind the shit getting beaten out of him and occasionally inflicts injuries on himself just to ride the pain, and he's fixated on passenger safety. Won't even start the car unless everyone's buckled up.

Yet another of his many quirks, I guess.

"Are you sure, man? Last time we did a pickup there were like six guys waiting for us, all armed."

Brick gives me a withering look. "Please. I've got this."

I shake my head and smirk as he checks his guns and closes the car door.

Brick's recklessness can be his downfall, but I've seen him take on more than six guys and come out grinning, plumes of smoke and destruction billowing in his wake.

These guys aren't anything like Tane's foot soldiers, so I'm not super worried about them, although of course it only takes one stray bullet to ruin your night or life.

He walks to the dimly lit door. He tugs on the door and it opens, and he slips inside the fortified building to pick up our items.

And now I wait.

CHAPTER 18

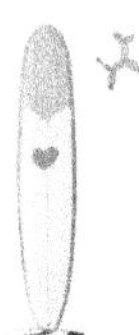

BRICK

t was cute when Slade offered to come into the warehouse with me. Fretting like he was a first-time dad, dropping his kid off on the first day of elementary school. Like he was mildly concerned I wouldn't be able to take on six guys.

Come on. I snort to myself as I open the warehouse door. It's dark inside at first, but then my eyes adjust, revealing a mostly empty warehouse with some dilapidated equipment sitting in the middle of the room.

I can tell straight away that the interior of the building is empty, which is a good start to this pickup.

It's not this part of the job that I'm most concerned about. None of what I do scares me. The more fucked up, the more twisted, the better, in my opinion. That's why I prefer torture to pickups like this.

But pickups have to be done, especially as we're quickly becoming this island's premiere transporter of illicit items. Most lowlifes are too scared to come to this neighborhood, because they know these compounds are usually heavily armed. They know we know what we're doing, and that we have intensive security protocols in place. It would be guaranteed suicide for all but the best.

It's when I leave the building shortly, and when Slade and I make it onto the road with our haul, that we'll need to be on our highest alert. We've been followed many times, picking stuff up from here and other drop points. The goods we transport are worth a lot of money, and people either want them to on-sell and profit from or to keep for themselves.

Scanning the room, I see the packages are exactly where they're meant to be. One is a long, hard-cased container, a bit like a narrow suitcase. The other is a large canvas duffel that's almost bursting at the seams.

I hoist the canvas bag over my shoulder and lift the case with my left hand, leaving my right hand free for my gun.

I don't think I'll need it today, but you never know.

As I emerge from the building, I look around as my eyes once again adjust to the night.

Approaching halfway between the building and the vehicle, I sense movement in my peripheral vision to my left. A glint of metal reflects the moonlight. One-handed, I turn and swing in that direction, shooting just beyond where I saw the metallic flash. I hear a groan and a figure dressed in black crumples to the ground.

Slade jumps out of the car, his gun drawn.

We do a perimeter check, our backs to each other, our weapons pointed. These guys never come alone. There has to be at least one more guy out here, maybe two.

The audacity of these lazy fuckers, having us negotiate and arrange the entire purchase and drop-off, and then trying to pick us off when we collect the goods.

The crackle of gunfire rings out, followed by a flash of light off in the distance, and we dive to the ground, scrambling to use the vehicle as a shield to protect us from the direction the shot was fired from.

"You go left," Slade whispers and I nod. We split off in opposite directions.

Creeping around the vehicle, we listen intently for any sign of men advancing toward us.

A bullet whistles past us and we smash ourselves into the ground. That was too close. But it told us all we needed to know.

From the direction the shot came from, two men run out of the trees and race for the bag and the case. I raise my gun, shooting them from where I'm laying down on my stomach, and drop both of them with ease. My silencer keeps things polite, my gun hardly making a noise as it ejects two deadly bullets. We listen for a while, but there are no further sounds except for nature.

We get up, and I grab the case and the bag and load them into the car. I grin at Slade. "Guns and drugs, baby. Guns and drugs!" We buckle our seatbelts and head out.

We drive back in silence, and after a while, I flick on the radio. I can't stand silence. It messes with my head and allows me to have thoughts that aren't healthy.

I know that Slade's the exact opposite. He needs silence and solitude. He craves it and when he doesn't get it for a while, his energy saps out of him.

It's ironic that he lives in a house with so many people, but we've done it for so long and we're so close that he seems to have found a way to tune us out, and it's almost like we don't count toward the noise that he avoids.

Despite his probably not wanting to listen to the radio, he doesn't try to touch it at first. Partway to the house, he can't take it anymore and clicks it off. The silence returns, just the sound of the car as it bounces along the highway. I glance at him. "You okay, man?"

"Yeah… well, no. I just don't know how we're going to deal with this girl in our space, even if it's just for a few days. We talk about sensitive stuff. We can't have her running off telling people our business."

"Yeah. And I mean, she also saw Roman murder someone. That's why she's with us in the first place. I've gotten used to her being around, even though it hasn't been that long. But you're right, she could overhear a lot of confidential information and then weaponize it against us."

"Look, I get you wanting to keep her around for a bit. It sounds like maybe you'll have your fun and then we'll have no choice. We shouldn't let it just drag on forever. The more she knows, the more dangerous she is."

I sigh and then nod in resignation. She might be pretty, but I have a feeling this isn't going to end that way. For her, or for any of us.

CHAPTER 19

ROMAN

The sun slowly sets until it's finally dark outside, which means it's time to think about tying up loose ends.

Aidan's mantra repeats on a loop in my mind, 'Dead ends, not loose ends. Dead ends, not loose ends.'

I don't know when he became my personal Jiminy Cricket. Level-headed and wise, sitting on my shoulder and guiding my decisions even when he's not actually there.

But unlike Jiminy, who focused on guiding Pinocchio down some over-hyped 'righteous path', Aidan's just here to make sure we don't screw anything up too badly. That we don't do anything that prevents us from amassing the wealth and power that we've worked so hard for. Whether we break a law or hurt somebody, or generally act in a way that some people would consider immoral, is of no consequence to him.

"I guess one of us should go and clean up the mess we left in the hair salon," says Aidan, as if reading my mind. Or maybe, seeing it's his voice I heard rattling around my brain, it was me reading his.

"Oh yeah. The huge puddle of blood and everything," says

Brick. "Not that I personally mind a splash of blood as an interior design aesthetic." He gets a dreamy look in his eyes, and his tongue flicks across his bottom lip. "When it splatters across the basement, sometimes I leave it there for a little bit. It helps to foreshadow events for the next person I bring in there for a party. Plus, did you know that blood's distinctive metallic smell is because of the oxidation of the hemoglobin's iron molecules? That they react with fat lipids in the skin?"

His outburst doesn't raise an eyebrow from any of us. We know Brick is like a walking encyclopedia when it comes to blood.

"Yeah, yeah, we get it, Brick," Aidan smirks. "If you could wear blood as an aftershave, you would. You'd bathe in it every day if you could."

"I wouldn't go that far," pouts Brick. "But I think it gets a bad rap. It's a versatile and fascinating substance that works well in a variety of artistic mediums."

"Okay, out of Brick's science and imagination emporium and back to reality," I clear my throat. If I don't stop him now, he'll continue like this for hours. "I closed the blinds up front at the salon," I remind them. "Still, we don't need anybody peeking in and asking questions. We should probably get rid of the mess now, in case someone somehow stumbles upon it and calls the cops. There's a lot of blood, too much blood to plausibly explain away."

"Shit, do we need to change the locks as well?" Aidan's face falls. He looks like he missed a beat for a moment, like he didn't check off every potential risk, which is unusual for him. "Does she have employees?"

"It's okay, Aidan. I've checked all this. She works alone," I say. "She told me."

"Somehow I get the feeling that doesn't just apply to her at the salon," snorts Slade.

"No cleaning contractors or anything like that to worry about, either?" Aidan raises an eyebrow.

"No, she's a lone wolf when it comes to that place. Does all the cleaning and other stuff herself."

"It sounds like she's stubborn and refuses to accept any help," says Brick.

"We're talking about cleaning a blood puddle, not analyzing her inbuilt psychological trauma," says Aidan, giving Brick a sideways glance. He turns his gaze to me. "Roman, you made the mess, so you should go take care of it."

"Since when has that been a rule? Don't we help each other out and not assign blame?" I prefer making messes to cleaning them up. Especially blood. It's so stubborn to clean because it sinks into everything.

"Since now," sighs Aidan. "It's been a rule since now. Slade's clearly pissed you brought her here in the first place. I have business to take care of here. If you can get Brick to go along with you, great. Otherwise, figure it out on your own. We won't always be around to help you clean up your problems."

"I could take *her* with me," I shrug.

"Who, Angel?" He squints at me like he thinks I'm an absolute lunatic. "No, nice try, Ro. You are *not* taking *her* with you. Jesus, Roman. She's not a little chihuahua that you can carry around in a dog bag. She's a fucking murder witness. You've brought her here, and now we have to figure out what to do with her. But we're not going to be parading her around everywhere we go, hoping she doesn't sing like a bird. It defeats the purpose of bringing her with us in the first place. People ask too many questions, and we need to keep her away from people."

Brick's eyes grow dreamy again. "Because she's feisty and violent and unpredictable, and she puts up a hell of a struggle when she wants to."

"Yes," says Aidan, "and we *don't fucking know her*." He punctuates the last words, exasperated by how quickly we've incorporated her into our house. Reminding us that it's been twenty-four hours, if that. "Listen. I know some of you are fine with her hanging out with us as if she's our roommate," he glances from

Brick to me. "But Slade is right to be cautious. She has the makings of someone who can stand up for herself and who doesn't take any shit. But we don't know what she's actually like. What information she's trying to get from us. How badly she wants to escape and the lengths she'll go to. Whether, if we ever let her go, she feels the need to turn us in and tell the authorities all about our business."

Slade scowls. "It's a real problem. I'm glad you're taking it seriously, Aid. I can think of one solution that would bring things to a permanent close."

"We're not killing her, Slade." Brick's eyes flash. "Not yet, anyway. I want to play with her first. She seems fun."

"Fine. I'll go take care of it alone." I roll my eyes. "I'm sure Brick has more important things to do and the rest of you are occupied. It's not like I need help to clean blood, anyway."

I've been hoping to spend more time with Angel, but the opportunities have been few and far between so far. I figured taking her with me to clean up the salon would give us some alone time together, and the opportunity for her to warm up to me some more. When I came up with the idea, there didn't seem to be much downside to having her accompany me on an other-wise boring job. But, as usual, Aidan comes and rains on my parade. Picking the safest option, the most conservative course of action. 'Protecting the brotherhood' as he would say.

Slade is, of course, egging him on, instigating all this talk of risk and distractions.

I'm frustrated as hell, but I need to get over it.

I'll just go knock this job out alone and then figure out another way to spend more time with her.

I'll ignore the fact I'm a grown-ass man who is being told I can't make a simple decision to take her on a low-risk job with me.

Aidan's probably right, as usual, but it doesn't mean I like it.

———

I drive north, leaving the industrial neighborhood to transition onto the freeway and then down into the residential area where her salon is located.

The roads are fairly quiet, the commuter traffic having long since trickled people back to their neighborhoods.

Island life, outside of a couple of hours in the mornings and afternoons, is relatively sleepy and predictable. You could live your life in a place like this completely oblivious to the seedy underbelly of criminal activity that goes on here.

You could live your life on this island without worrying that folks like me and my brothers exist.

But when you do want trouble, when you scratch under the surface of the sunshine and the lush green vegetation, the tourist artifice and the high-end retail and front-facing restaurant culture, we're back here doing our thing.

And it's just as dark and gritty here as what you might find in any city back on the mainland.

Everything might seem curated, beautiful, magical.

But put a foot wrong around here with the wrong people, and danger and death become imminent.

It's no different from anywhere else. And in some cases, it's much worse.

When I reach the salon, I pull around back and park the vehicle. Getting out of the car, my body tenses and the little hairs stand up on the back of my neck.

Something is off. My instincts are pretty good about this kind of thing.

Unholstering my gun, I approach the salon and enter through the back door. It's dark inside, but my eyes quickly adjust.

I am alone in here, but things are not at all as we left them.

Far from it.

The entire place has been ransacked, and I thought I'd made a mess yesterday, but now my efforts look like child's play.

Instead of the blood puddle being the center of attention in the middle of the salon, the entire place has been torn to pieces.

Cabinets have been thrown over, their contents sprawling over the ground. Files of documents and cleaning supplies spill out onto the floor, ripped and torn.

Tubes of brown and red hair dye have been squirted and smeared over just about every surface—walls, the floor, even the ceiling. It looks like someone has covered the place in blood and shit, like in some gruesome horror movie. I can't show this to Brick or he might try to decorate his room like this.

Sharp scissors have been violently stabbed into the wall, with only their handles protruding. It reminds me a little bit of what I did to The Asshole's neck.

Angel's hairstyling and business diplomas and certificates have been ripped from their frames, the glass smashed and the documents torn into pieces and sprinkled over the floor.

Looking around at the destruction, my immediate thought is that this must be some type of warning from whoever sent The Asshole to find me. They must have come looking for him when he didn't report back.

But then I see the message that's been left by whoever did this. Sprayed across the long salon mirror is *'Die Slut Bitch! I'll Finish What I Started. I'm Coming For You.'*

This note doesn't seem meant for me. The timing seems coincidental as I read that. I mean, technically the 'finishing what they started' piece could ring true for my little murder situation, but the die slut bitch piece doesn't compute. I've been called many things by many people, but that would be a new one.

This can't be about what happened here earlier. This seems to be more about... her. About Angel. But who would destroy her salon like this?

I survey the scene one more time, from the lens that whoever did this was trying to get to Angel rather than send me a message.

It makes the room feel different when the destruction is aimed at her. More personal somehow.

A chill creeps up my back. My chest and back muscles tighten involuntarily, and I clench my jaw.

I text the guys on our group chat:

Me:Get here now. I need you to see this for yourselves.

Brick:Jeez, bro. Can't you visit the hair salon without needing us to hold your hand? That'll be the second time.

Me:Not the time for jokes. Get here now.

Aidan:We can't just leave her here by herself.

Me:Bring her then.

Aidan:No way. She's not leaving the house.

Me:Well, two of you come here then and someone can stay behind to look after her.

Slade:I'll stay here and keep an eye on her.

Aidan:Alright. Be there shortly.

Me:Don't you lay a finger on her, Slade. (glaring emoji)

Slade:If she doesn't do anything to deserve it, I won't. (shrug emoji)

Brick:Don't touch her, man. (swearing emoji)

Slade:Whatever. See how she's making you behave? Distracting AF. (eye roll emoji)

Aidan:Enough. See you soon, Roman.

I use my phone to snap some photos of the scene in front of me.

Whoever did this is clearly unhinged. Full of rage when they carried out this overwhelming destruction.

Not that any of us can talk. It takes an unhinged person to truly recognize another. But it's like whoever did this completely lost their mind in this room. As if they entered an alternate reality where their sole focus was to erase her, to annihilate everything she's worked so hard for. To inflict maximum damage.

This wasn't a crime of opportunity or a petty act by someone who was mildly pissed. This wasn't done by a client not happy with their hair treatment, someone whose bangs were cut too short or whose trim was uneven. The perpetrator, whoever did this, has some type of emotional attachment to Angel. I wonder if it's a scorned ex, or maybe an estranged family member.

Within about ten minutes there's a knock at the back door, and part of me hopes it's whatever psycho did this coming back for round two. I'd really like to take care of him, show him a good time at the end of my gun for what they've done to the salon that Angel has worked so hard for. Fucking hell, I might even need to find another hair salon to go to because of this. Not again.

But then again, I wouldn't expect whoever did this to knock if they did return, and it's not like they could cause more destruction here than they already have.

I head to the back and let Brick and Roman in, like I did the first time I called them here. We're just missing Slade this time around. Which is fine, because he'd just spend the entire time reminding us that he thinks we should have knocked Angel off and buried her in the woods next to The Asshole.

If Aidan is my conscience on my shoulder, Slade is an enneagram six with a five-wing dancing around on my deltoid, always thinking several steps ahead to anticipate what could go wrong. On a constant tightrope of perceiving threats, imaginary and real, and withdrawing completely within his own thoughts.

We don't need his energy right now.

I gesture to the main part of the salon and they head on through.

Brick lets out a low whistle as he surveys the damage. "Jesus, someone really went to town on this place. I was expecting another dead body and maybe hoping for another unconscious hot chick, but this is something else." He glances around, taking it all in. "Retribution for what you did to their guy, do you think?"

Aidan shakes his head. "Definitely not. That's not what this is about."

"How do you figure?" asks Brick.

"There are two reasons why not." Aidan holds up two fingers.

"Oh, yeah?" I'm curious. I could only think of one.

"There's no dead body here. No obvious evidence tying the dead guy to this salon. It's not like anyone came in here and took DNA that leads back to you. If someone did see the blood, it's not like they know who it belonged to. He followed you in yesterday. It's not like you had a longstanding appointment, right?"

I nod. He has a point.

"This... whatever this is," says Aidan, gesturing around at the mess, "it wasn't intended to spook you, Roman. I don't think you crossed the mind of whoever did this. I'd guess that you're not even on their radar."

I nod. "You don't think I'm the slut to which the note is referring?" I grin, pointing at the scrawled writing sprayed on the smashed mirror.

"Don't get me wrong, Roman, you are a complete and utter slut so if the message was about you it would be accurate," shrugs Aidan, missing the humor in my question. "But I don't think someone would come and spray paint that about you at this place you've had no prior ties to."

"So what then?"

"Clearly, this person is fixated on whoever runs this place, or at least someone who works here."

"And she works by herself. She made that abundantly clear. Which means..." my voice trails off, the implications settling in.

"Someone wants to hurt Angel. Someone is this angry at her about something?" Brick scowls and crossed his arms tightly over his muscular chest. "I mean, it's one thing if we want to hurt her for fun, but this pisses me off. There's hate in these actions."

A thought strikes me. "We should check on her apartment. Make sure it's secure. Maybe this isn't the only place he visited."

The other guys nod.

"First let's clean up the blood puddle though, man," says Aidan. "Someone could still come in. And who knows how much noise was made while whoever it was destroyed this place. We should probably hurry in case the cops have already been called."

He's so logical, pragmatic, always noticing the details that would otherwise trip us up. If you'd left it to me and Brick, we would have up and left the salon in a race to get to her apartment.

We'd be lost without him. He keeps us focused. We need him.

I head outside and retrieve the bleach and rags from the car and bring them back inside, making sure to lock the car. We don't need to recreate some slasher flick where we're driving and a lunatic with a knife appears in the back of the vehicle.

We get to work removing the bloodstain, and I'm glad the other two guys have joined me because it takes more elbow grease than I anticipated. The blood has settled into cracks in the linoleum and splattered onto some cabinets nearby, and it takes a while to get all the dark red stains out.

For good measure, Aidan has Brick 'decorate' the freshly cleaned area with the same type of crazy artwork that adorns the rest of the salon's surfaces. He surveys the rest of the destruction like he's an aficionado at a fine art museum, and then he picks up various tubes and spray bottles and gets to work. He swirls and smears, festooning the area in a cacophony of artful lines and swishes and strokes. By the time he's done, Brick has managed to replicate someone else's unadulterated chaos, and it blends in seamlessly. Nobody would ever guess that a man died in this particular spot, or that it hadn't been created by the same person who 'decorated' the rest of the space.

We're pleased with the finished outcome, even though it's like the reverse of a TV show where some celebrity host comes and turns your business around for the better. Angel won't be having any clients here any time soon, and I'd hazard a guess that this place is not insured.

After locking up, we hop into our vehicles and ride to Angel's address.

I pull into the apartment complex moments before Aidan and Brick. Wasting no time, we leap out of the vehicles and clamber up the stairs to her apartment two at a time, following Brick's lead. As we approach the entrance, it's immediately clear that all is not okay here, either. The door has been kicked open and is dangling from its hinges.

From here, the inside of the apartment looks just as bad as the salon, but with different stuff strewn around. The detritus of an apartment versus a workplace, turned inside out for all to see.

"Well, shit. You said she was messy, but this is another level," I smirk as I glance around the disaster zone.

"What I saw before was a two out of ten on this scale," Brick says, shaking his head. "She's messy, but she's not dirty, from what I could tell."

"Oh, she's dirty," smirks Aidan. "You're reading her wrong."

"That's not what I'm talking about, Aidan," huffs Brick. "You're lucky Slade isn't here to hear you joke like that. He would have gone off."

"I know. I'm just giving you shit while I try to process what this means. Two locations hit in one day. Let's go in and assess the extent of the damage. See if we can find out anything about who might have done this."

We make our way inside, our feet crunching on various items that have been smashed into the floor.

In the living room, pictures and art have been ripped off the wall, the glass smashed, and the artwork torn just like her diplomas back at the salon.

She has a photo wall that celebrates happier times with what appears to be family and friends, and someone has gone to the trouble of scratching out her eyes in every single photo. A violent erasure of her gorgeous eyes that seem to have seen so much.

Her TV has been shattered, the screen smashed and the entire appliance thrown onto the floor. Her clothes have been pulled from her dresser and strewn about.

Brick picks up a couple of items. "Jesus, whoever did this took the time to chop up her clothing with something sharp."

Sure enough, the items he's holding have been slashed in multiple places.

In her bedroom, her bed has been stabbed repeatedly, tufts of filler floating out of the ravaged mattress.

Her floor-length mirror has been smashed into hundreds of shards, some larger pieces embedded in the mattress and pillows.

We move down the hallway into the kitchen, where knives have been stabbed through the walls with the same rage as the scissors in the salon.

What is with this stabbing of walls? Who does this? Clearly someone with a lot of rage directed at Angel.

Contents from her fridge and pantry have been poured and squirted out, leaving a nasty, sticky mess on just about every surface. We have to walk carefully so that we don't slip on the slick coating left behind by sauces and liquids and condiments.

Ants have discovered the sticky mess and started to tell their ant friends, a thin line of thousands of them marching back and forth between the goo and presumably a crack in the wall that connects them with their nest on the outside.

On the other side of the hall, the bathroom is no better. And just like at the salon, it has a message spray-painted on the mirror.

"You can't escape me. I'm coming for you, bitch. I have been waiting for this."

"Jesus," says Brick, letting out another low whistle. "Someone really has it in for her."

"We have to go home. We have to tell her," I say.

Aidan looks around one more time and nods. "Let's go. We have to figure out what this is all about. We need to talk to Angel. She has to know who hates her this much."

CHAPTER 20

ANGEL

They've left me with Slade, the quiet one who seems to do all the cooking. The one who knows me least but hates me most, judging by the way he constantly scowls at me.

I'm torn, though, because he's so hot when he scowls. There's something about the way his eyes darken and his lip curls that's primal, and it does things to me.

"You shouldn't be here, you know." I know he's talking to me, but he doesn't make eye contact, instead cleaning imaginary debris off the counter.

Being in the kitchen seems to be a security blanket for him, giving him something to do, something to focus on, without having to sit down next to everyone else.

"You think I want to be here? If you recall, it wasn't exactly my choice," I remind him. He acts as if I forced myself upon them, somehow sneaking my way under their roof, instead of being brought here while unconscious, against my will.

"We should have killed you back at the salon," he says, matter-of-factly, like he's not talking about whether he and the other guys should have murdered me just because I was in the wrong place at the wrong time. "It would have been cleaner. Everyone would have been better off."

Charming.

I can't help but let out a hollow laugh.

"You're probably right," I shrug. "The world probably would be better off without me. So kill me if you want. I don't care. Just hurry up and do it. Part of me already died a long time ago."

He stops wiping the counter and peers at me. "You really mean that?"

"Yeah, sure," I shrug again. "If you don't, somebody else probably will soon, anyway."

"Wait, what do you mean?" He's standing up straight now, confused.

"It's nothing." I close my eyes and sigh.

I don't want to think about it. I shouldn't have said what I did. It was obviously going to lead to questions.

"Tell me," he says, hanging the dishtowel up on the handle of the oven.

"Tell you what?"

He sighs. "Why you're sad or scared or whatever you are. And why you think somebody is going to kill you." He peers at me. "Other than us, I mean."

"I'm not sad or scared." It's a lie on both counts, but he doesn't need to know how I'm feeling inside. It'll just give him more reason to hate me.

"Then why did you just look like you were holding back tears? Why do you think you're going to die soon?"

"I had something in my eye," I say weakly. "Stop pushing me. Leave it."

"Look. You clearly have stuff you don't want to tell me, and that's fine. But I recognize the way you're looking around, trying to pretend nothing's wrong while your mind is racing to fix whatever it is. You're clearly full of pain. I recognize it in you."

"Oh yeah? And how the fuck would you recognize that?" I snap, and I know my eyes are flashing.

But instead of pulling away like most people do when I lash out, Slade walks up to me.

He grabs me by my upper arms and pushes me further into the kitchen until my back presses up against the refrigerator. He takes hold of both of my wrists, placing them against the fridge on either side of my head, and gazes into my eyes.

My pulse leaps as I feel his body press into mine and I feel the same crackle of electricity as when we sat next to each other for dinner, but our proximity makes it more intense now as the full lengths of our bodies touch. He's solid muscle, and I like the way he melds into my curves.

"Maybe I recognize it in you because it's like I'm holding up a mirror when I look at you," he growls. "Maybe you look the way I feel inside."

"You don't know the first thing about me. You're a fucking kidnapper." I narrow my eyes at him, but my voice stays eerily calm.

How dare he think he can read me, that he can possibly understand how I'm feeling? He hasn't even tried to get to know me. He's clearly assumed the worst about me and doesn't want me to be here.

"You'd be surprised what I know, Angel," he says, his eyes growing dark, a twinge of what might be sadness clouding them for a moment. "Sometimes it's not words that tell you the most about someone."

He removes a hand from one of my wrists and traces the line of my jaw with a long finger. His hand is rough, but he's gentle, and it sends a little bolt of electricity down my neck, leaving me tingling.

"Oh, really?" I roll my eyes, but I can't help my body arching into his, my softness blending with his hardness, seeking him out, hungry for him to press further into me.

He bites his lip and groans softly. "Yes, really," he rasps, and he crushes his lips down on mine, hard. I know they'll be bruised later, but I mash mine into his right back.

I feel a twinge between my legs as he swipes his tongue through my lips and explores my mouth. I reciprocate, my tongue wrapping around his, and I involuntarily let out a moan as he twirls his tongue against mine.

I feel wet heat pooling at my entrance as he continues pressing his strong body against me, as if my body is craving him, craving more of this unique connection we have.

Through our clothes, I can tell he's hard and that he's big. It's like an iron bar is pressing firmly into my stomach. For someone that hates me, I've sure got his attention.

Continuing to hold one of my wrists above my head, he reaches down with his other strong hand and cups my heat. I let out another soft moan, longing for him to touch my bare skin and to be inside me.

If he could channel his palpable hatred for me into the bedroom, his intense emotional distress at my presence, that could really be something. In this moment, I want nothing more than for him to fuck me with the energy of the scowls he constantly sends my way.

Suddenly, he pulls away, and the hand he was holding against the refrigerator drops to my side. He backs off, moving toward the counter.

Fucking hell.

I glare at him.

"Why'd you stop?" I ask. "Am I not good enough for you?" I don't handle rejection well. "I don't make you hard enough? Were the other guys right that you can't get it up?"

Slade's scowl has returned. He glares at me. "Fuck you, Angel. I told you that you shouldn't be here."

He stomps off into the other room.

A moment later he returns, probably remembering he's meant to be keeping an eye on me and he can't leave me with access to the front door.

Before I can say anything else to offend him, he picks me up, hauls me over his shoulder and carries me up the stairs. I ball my hands into fists and pummel him on the back and try to kick him, but he doesn't say anything. He just continues to carry me, silently, in his strong arms, as if I'm an annoying object rather than a person.

He brings me up the stairs and down the hallway to my room, lowers me onto the bed and immediately leaves as if he doesn't want to be in there alone with me.

The lock in the door clicks, and I hear his footsteps retreating back down the stairs.

So here I am again, alone in my room.

Turned on by Slade.

Frustrated that I'm turned on by Slade.

Confused by why he got me all worked up and then abruptly pulled away.

Confused by why he hates me so much when he barely knows me.

Thrown off by his words right before he kissed me.

What is his fucking deal?

CHAPTER 21

ROMAN

On the ride home, I keep thinking about the destruction we just saw.

There's no question that the person who did this is extremely unhinged and obsessed with Angel.

The way they destroyed her salon and her apartment, the two spaces that are uniquely hers, was very methodical even in its chaos. And all of it was deeply, deeply personal.

The messages, the way they went to great lengths to leave a stain on nearly every surface. Scratching her eyes out in photographs. Stabbing the walls in both locations.

This is no petty crime of opportunity. This is intentional. This is about Angel, specifically. And this person wants to destroy her, to erase her, to inflict maximum pain.

I might not know Angel well, but this makes me feel protective of her. She doesn't deserve to have someone invade her most private of places. The way they'd rifled through her drawers and broken things just because they could. Basically tipped her life all over the floor and ripped it apart. Everything she's worked hard for, based on what I know.

I shudder as I think about what might have happened if she'd been at home or at work when they stopped by. It seems obvious that they were displacing the anger they felt toward her onto both properties in her absence.

When we get home, I let her out of her bedroom. Slade apparently didn't know what to do with her, so locked her back in there.

Telling her we need to talk with her about something serious, I lead her downstairs to the living room and sit her down on the couch, and plop down next to her.

Without saying a word, I show her the photos of the salon on my phone.

Her face turns ashen and her eyes grow large, but it only lasts a second. Just as quickly, her eyes narrow and become flinty, and she clenches her jaw, grinding her teeth.

She clearly knows who did this, and she's in a visible tug-of-war between fear and anger.

"There's more," I say softly, showing her the photos of the apartment. "They were there, too."

Her face pales further, and she swallows hard, blinking back tears as she squints at the photos.

"My *place*. My apartment?" Her voice cracks and her chest rises and falls with urgency. She takes my phone and zooms in for a closer look. "He was there as well?" she whispers.

"I'm afraid so," I say, my voice gentle.

"No, no, no," she whispers. "He can't be out. He can't know where I am. How did he find me?"

"Who's he?" I ask.

"You know who did this, don't you, Angel?" Aidan asks, peering at her.

She doesn't reply, and her face is stony. Her eyes seem to focus on a random spot halfway across the room while her mind races, processing what she's just seen and what it means.

"Angel. Who did this?" Aidan repeats.

She adjusts her shoulders, pushing them back proudly, but

her voice is still low and it wavers as she speaks. "It doesn't matter. Nobody important. It's nothing I can't handle."

Despite her attempt at bravery, I detect a slight tremble in her chin. I look down and notice that her hands are also shaking. She sees me looking and balls them into fists so she can hold them still. I wonder if she's pressing her fingernails into her palms the way I do when I try to distract myself with pain.

She blinks rapidly, her eyes watering, and she flattens her lips together into a thin line. She crosses her arms tightly over her chest like a shield. Her body language is betraying her lack of verbal cues, and while she isn't putting it into words, I can literally see her turmoil.

A little piece of me melts seeing her like this, a little of her vulnerability peeking out. She's shown us that she's capable of being so strong and feisty, and yet the acts of this person have clearly shaken her to her core.

"Angel, we can help you," I say, lightly touching her shoulder.

She shrugs me off and turns away so that I can't see her face. She sighs and her shoulders drop, and she stills for a moment.

Suddenly, her shoulders rear back and she swivels around to face me, her breathing quick and shallow and her eyes wide.

"*You* can help me? The same people who kidnapped me? Especially the guy who came into my workplace and *murdered* someone while I stood there?" She glares at me, her eyes wild.

"If you thought that was bad for business, it's got nothing on what whoever this person is went and did to your salon. Or to your place."

Her face falls further.

"Who are they, Angel?" asks Aidan. "I'm assuming it's a he. Is he the same person who gave you those scars?"

She flinches at the mention of the marks on her body, as if whatever was done to cause her scars is being done to her all over again.

"It doesn't matter who he is," she says softly, blinking back tears.

"Tell us, Angel," I say, putting a hand on hers and holding it still. "Tell us what you know so we can help you."

"He's a ghost," she whispers, her voice barely audible.

Her body quakes with a held-in sob as she rushes from the room.

CHAPTER 22

ANGEL

An intense flood of nausea sweeps through my body. I run in the direction of the bathroom, but don't make it all the way to the toilet or sink in time.

Dropping to all fours, I heave the contents of my stomach onto the cold tile floor, and I wretch and shudder as the contents of my stomach are violently expelled.

Gasping for breath, my throat coils into a tight and scratchy little tube, causing me to gag. My eyes water and my chest pounds, both from my racing heart and the exertion of vomiting.

Panting, I stay where I am for a moment, fighting to regain my breath, looking at the mess in front of me. My body feels cold and clammy, the cold tiles like ice against my splayed fingers that tremble under my weight, barely holding me up.

I can't believe he's out. He was meant to be locked up for a lot longer. Decades.

I'm not surprised he managed to find a way out earlier than anticipated. It was a given that he'd find some way to buck the system, to turn things to his advantage.

But this? This is unimaginably early. It feels like it was just yesterday that he went in, and I always assumed I'd have a lot more time.

I'm sure that he used the same manipulative techniques he used on me, found all the loopholes the justice system provided, and took advantage.

That's how he operates.

Part of me always knew he would find me one day, that he would track me down no matter how far I ran or how careful I was. And I've lived with the idea that one unexpected day in the future I'd probably die at his hands.

Right before he was sentenced for his unspeakable crimes, and he got to say a few words in the courtroom, he didn't spend it communicating his remorse for his evil doings. He didn't pretend that he was sorry for the pain that he caused so many people, including me. He didn't try to say just the right things to minimize his sentence, either.

Instead, he locked eyes on me and told the entire courtroom that he and I were destined to be together, that he would spend every moment in prison thinking about me, and that the moment he got out of prison he would do nothing except focus on hunting me down.

He started going into detail about what he'd already done to me and what he would do to me when he got out, resulting in gasps from the courtroom as he detailed the horrific acts he had obsessed over and written about.

He delighted in detailing the joy that he experienced when he marked my body with a roadmap of scars, vividly describing each of the implements and techniques he used to craft each one, and the meaning behind them.

One person fainted as he talked about his plans for me once he got out.

In the end, he was dragged out by several wardens, his words too evil and lengthy for the room to bear. He was supposed to use the moment to gain sympathy, and some mercy from the judge and the jury, but he used the moment as a soliloquy on his obsession with me and his dark plans for my torturous death.

As they dragged him out of the courtroom, he turned his head to look behind him, locking eyes with me once more. His face had twisted into an icy smirk as he passed through the doors leading back to the jail, because he always knew he would find me again, no matter how hard I tried to hide.

"See you soon," he yelled, calling me by the name I grew up with.

Not Angel. Angel is a new development that he wasn't meant to ever find out about. But it's clearly too late to worry about that now. That ship has well and truly sailed.

He's seen the salon named after me. He's been in my home and no doubt seen letters addressed to me. He must have found out my new name long before to even track me down here. So much for being undercover.

So it's not a surprise that he's managed to find me. It's just happened much sooner than I thought it would.

I thought I'd done a good job of burning the remnants of my prior life. No attachments to my family, because he killed them all, so that part was 'easy', relatively speaking.

The same goes for close friends back on the mainland. He eliminated anyone I cared about. Some he took from the earth, the ones who insisted on remaining in my life no matter how difficult it might have been to be my friend. The ones who would send me messages and invite me out for coffee even when I said no for the hundredth time.

The others, the more fair-weather friends, he surgically isolated me from until they decided our friendship took too much effort and they naturally floated away to greener pastures, to friends who would give them the attention they so desperately craved.

Now he's eliminated everyone in his path, and he's after the grand finale. Me.

I took precautions so that he wouldn't find me, or at least so that it would take him extra time. I changed my name, and I drastically changed my appearance. New ID, new phone, new bank accounts, new wardrobe, everything new. A self-made version of a witness protection identity change.

I don't tell people very much about me. I don't chat with people online. My life here on this island has consisted of work at the salon, quiet time at my apartment, and making the odd friend who lives a quiet life here.

And surfing a few times a week, which is about as off the grid as you can get. No phones, no cameras. Just the ocean, my board, and me.

There's no way a normal human being could have tracked me down here. This has to have taken considerable focus and resources. Then again, as he's proven time and time again, he's far from normal and incredibly resourceful. Regular barriers don't stand in his way.

Unfortunately, obsession and evil sometimes find a path when it doesn't seem possible.

And I am the object of his fixation. He won't rest until he kills me, and he's made it clear it will be a torturous and excruciating death.

I hear a noise behind me and flinch at the sensation of a hand pressing against my back.

My mental box of dark thoughts snaps closed and I'm suddenly back to reality, on all fours in the bathroom, hovering over a disgusting pile of vomit.

"Angel," a voice says softly. It's Aidan, his hand on my back. "Let me help you up."

He extends his hand and I grab it. He pulls me to my feet and glances at the puddle of vomit on the floor as he helps me out of the room.

"Yo, Brick!" he calls out down the hallway. "Cleanup on Aisle Three!"

"Got you, boss!" Brick's voice carries back down the hallway and I hear him get up to go get supplies.

I glance at myself in the mirror. My complexion is paler than usual, and my eyes are still watery and bloodshot. My face is puffy. I'm a mess on the outside, but none of it compares to how I'm feeling on the inside.

I don't know how I'm going to make it through this. If I even want to make it through. I'm just so very tired of it all, and feeling incredibly beaten down and unprepared for what's yet to come.

"Let's go sit down," says Aidan, his arm around me, concern in his eyes.

He leads me to the living room and takes a seat beside me on the couch. Slade and Roman are sitting down as well, also observing me with concern.

"What's happening, Angel?" asks Roman, his eyes exploring mine for clues.

"Tell us so we can figure out what to do," says Slade. His tone isn't what sympathetic sounds like for most people, but it probably is for him. His version of care and concern, at least.

He's probably equally worried about how whatever this situation is might affect him and his brotherhood, but I can't blame him for that. None of them asked me to bring my problems into their lives. And I have some deep, dark problems including a sadistic madman hellbent on ending my existence.

"You only need to tell us as much as you're comfortable with, Angel," says Aidan, putting his hand on top of mine. "Take your time. We're here for you."

I take a deep breath. I've been burned before, telling this story, and I'm not going to risk going into all the details again.

But I'm ready to share more with them than I've shared with anyone in a very long time.

CHAPTER 23

AIDAN

"He was someone that I used to know," she says, her voice soft and low. "He used to do really bad things to hurt me, and to hurt others." Her voice trembles slightly, and she speaks slowly as if she's testing the waters with her words.

She pauses, deep in thought, and I wait for her to continue. She seems hollow, spooked. Like if I make a slight move the wrong way she might jump out of her skin or shatter into delicate pieces. Her face is pale and her eyes seem haunted as she bubbles up memories that clearly were shoved down somewhere deep inside her mind.

"He must be out of prison now, obviously, although he wasn't meant to be released for a long time. I always worried that would happen. He's so manipulative, I knew he'd trick the justice system and get an early release. I just didn't realize it would be this soon."

She takes a deep breath, steeling herself to continue, and I squeeze her hand, keeping it on top of hers for comfort.

Slade's eyes narrow, his eyebrows furrowing in concentration as he listens. For once, it seems like he's scowling at the story rather than at her.

Roman leans forward intently, sitting on the edge of his seat, taking in every last word.

Brick returns, having completed his vomit cleanup duty. He silently takes a seat on the arm of the chair across from the couch, his gaze exploring the tense, anguished expression on Angel's face.

"He always said he'd track me down. I thought I'd found the perfect place to escape, that he'd never find me once I abandoned my old life and created a new one here on the island. It seemed like it was far enough away that there wouldn't be any loose ends, any breadcrumbs for him to follow."

She sighs, her haunted and bloodshot eyes meeting mine.

"But I guess he has found me here after all. He's clever and resourceful and he's never going to give up. I'm never going to be able to escape him, except through death. Even in death, there are things he said he'd do to my human form."

Her face screws into a grimace and she half-gags, as if she's visualizing him doing what she just described. She clutches at herself with both arms, as if she's trying to hold herself together. As if she might fall apart the moment she stopped squeezing.

I have the urge to reach out to her and pull her closer to me, to tell her she doesn't need to say any more. But part of me needs her to keep going, to tell the parts of her story that she feels able to tell right in this moment.

Roman opens his mouth as if to speak, but then closes it again, letting her continue to have the floor.

Slade and Brick's eyes stay fixed on her, their body language still.

"I always knew it would end this way, but I really thought I had a lot more time." She squeezes her eyes shut as if she's holding in tears. Her skin is flushed and coated in a soft sheen. "I just can't believe he's out and that he's already found me."

Brick's jaw is taut and I can almost hear his teeth grinding all the way from the armchair.

My chest tightens as she tells her story, even though I sense we're getting the abbreviated version.

My takeaway is that a crazed lunatic stalked her back on the mainland and said he'd find her again one day and kill her. And now he's here ready to follow through on his promise.

No wonder she's terrified. He sounds like a psycho. Which is a little ironic given who she's been staying with under the same roof.

We've seen the type of destruction he's capable of at both her salon and apartment.

She stops talking and looks down at the ground, twisting her fingers around each other. I wait, giving her space to continue, but no more words come.

That's all she will share for now.

We sit in silence. I'm processing what she just told us and what it means, and I'm sure the other guys are, too.

Brick puts a hand to his face, rubbing his lips, and I can almost see the wheels turning in his head.

She was concise as she described what happened, but I know that beneath the condensed story are no doubt many layers of trauma, many more details she's not yet ready to share. Maybe she never will be. The fear of being hunted by someone who will follow her to the ends of the earth. The length of time that this person has had such a hold over her.

She doesn't need to say it, but it's pretty clear this person is the reason behind most, if not all, of the scars that lace themselves across her entire body.

Even though she offers limited details about what she's been dealing with, it would be a lot for anybody to deal with.

She looks up, almost flinching as if she's expecting to see us staring at her with judgement. Her shoulders settle slightly when all that gazes back at her is concern and care, even from Slade.

She goes to speak but then stops. I can sense her working herself back up to the somewhat hysterical state she was just in. Her chest rises and falls rapidly, and she starts to clench and unclench her fists again as if forcing herself to speak.

"It's okay, Angel," I say, gently, in an attempt to soothe her. "You don't have to tell us everything right now."

I rub her back with a firm hand, and she gently presses herself into my palm.

Roman reaches over me and puts his hand on her knee, and gives it a light squeeze.

"It's okay, Angel, it's okay," he says softly. "You're safe here with us. We'll protect you."

I wrap my arm around her and pull her close to me, and feel her body trembling against mine.

Slade's eyes are fixed on her, a strange look on his face. It's not the usual anger I see directed her way by him. It's almost like he's seeing her for the first time, the way the rest of us have from the beginning.

"Am I really safe here with you?" she whispers, her eyes large and vacant, her body tense.

It's a loaded question. I don't know if she's asking if we'll keep her safe from her stalker, or if she's safe from us. In either case, it's a fair question.

She didn't choose to come here, didn't choose to watch Roman murder a man. Didn't choose for this stalker to fall into a deadly obsession with her and follow her to the ends of the earth vowing to destroy her.

Telling her we'll protect her probably rings a bit hollow in either case.

Despite the unusual circumstances, I mean every word I say.

I will protect her, at all costs.

I've seen so many emotions in Angel already. I've seen fear, anger, confusion, and even a little lust.

But now I just see her terror, and I'm determined to make it go away.

CHAPTER 24

BRICK

"What are we going to do now?" My heart is racing, and my nostrils flare uncontrollably, my deep exhales sending flickers of cool air across my beard.

I crack my knuckles in an attempt to calm myself, but it only makes me more agitated. I want to use them now, for my knuckles to shatter the skull of the psycho that's hunting our Angel.

Angel has left the living room, leaving the four of us reeling from what she just shared. She said she wasn't feeling well and wanted to lie down. Nobody can blame her after both what she told us and the effort it took to share it.

She was visibly drained by the time she gave us a high-level overview, as if she was beaten down by having to relive her dark memories. All I want is to heal her pain, but all I could do at that moment was listen as she bared her soul.

Roman walked her up to her room with a glass of water, and apparently, she just climbed into the bed and pulled the covers over her entire body including her face. I can't blame her for wanting to hide, for wanting to shut this all out until it's over.

It's been a wild few days for our houseguest, through no fault of her own, and with the unanticipated arrival of a psycho stalker on the island, it seems things are only getting started.

I'm so fucking furious that someone would destroy her property the way he did. Destroying every little thing that meant anything to her, shredding and slashing and carving and snapping until everything was gone. Useless. Damaged. Dead.

I shiver as I imagine what might have happened if she'd been at home or work by herself when that monster swung by. I'm pretty sure the scissors and the knives would have ended up embedded in her flesh instead of the wall. The wall was just a proxy to absorb a tiny sliver of the hate this monster harbors toward her.

I want to take whoever this guy is down into my basement and spend hours alone with him. Days even, maybe entire weeks if I can work slowly and precisely enough, inflicting maximum pain with minimum damage as I mimic his every shred and slash and carve and snap all over his body.

There will be no mercy shown. I'll sear his eyeballs in his skull while he shrieks in terror, removing his ability to look at Angel, to come after her anymore. So that he quakes in terror as he sightlessly wonders what tool I'll use to torture him next.

I will not let him rest, even when his body and mind try to give up and let him escape into a world of unconsciousness.

I will keep him awake until every last drop of blood trickles from his body, until he is nothing but a flaccid pile of gored flesh and shattered bones.

I'll string his tendons across the ceiling beams like they're streetlights.

And I will do it while she watches.

My Angel, my Valkyrie. Watching me as I bring her tormentor to his knees, to his own merciless, torturous death. Nothing could be too dark, too depraved, for him to deserve.

The things I plan on doing to him will be the first time my monster is truly unleashed. Everyone around here thinks they know me, but they haven't seen the true depths of my darkness, where I'm truly willing to go.

"Come back to us, Brick," I hear Slade's voice. "Brick," he says again.

I feel a hand on my shoulder, shaking me. I snap back to the present, my eyes darting to the person connected to the arm on my shoulder.

It's Slade.

That was a risky move on his part, bringing me back to reality when I'm in the middle of a torture daydream, the rush of blood ringing in my ears, my bloodlust settling in.

I've been told I growl when I'm like that, that it's animalistic. From the way my throat feels a bit raw I'm guessing I just did it again, too.

My chest is tight, my heart is racing and my jaw is stiff from grinding my teeth as I listened to Angel share her demons.

"Thanks for bringing me back, man," I say, shaking my head. "I went somewhere."

"You sure did," Slade nods and returns to his seat.

Aidan runs a hand through his close-cropped dark hair, a sure sign that he's thinking intently. Knowing him, he's considered about five scenarios already and narrowed them down to the optimal plan to deal with the situation."There's only one thing I think we can do," he says with a sigh.

I feel a bit sick when I hear him say that, a knot the size of a large fist appearing in my stomach. I think I know what he's going to suggest. "You want to kill her first, before the psycho does? Save her the pain that he has planned for her?" I exhale, my shoulders slumping in defeat. I don't want to hurt Angel like that, but if it saves her from suffering at the hands of a psycho I'll do what needs to be done.

I'll show her mercy, make it quick and painless, the opposite of how I usually treat people who end up in my basement for one reason or another.

"I think that's a good idea," Slade nods enthusiastically, more engaged in this conversation than most. "Then we can go back to normal and the psycho can slither off and find someone else to obsess over. Or we could kill him for sport once she's gone. From what she's shared, it sounds like he deserves it." He shrugs and looks at Aidan as if he's expecting him to be in full agreement.

"No, that's not what I meant!" Aidan shakes his head and furrows his brow. "I wasn't suggesting we kill her. Far from it. What's wrong with you two? Jesus."

"Yeah, what the fuck, guys? You're both fucking psychos," says Roman, frowning at me and then Slade. "I vote we need to keep her and protect her and find the son of a bitch who did this and flay his skin from his body and feed it to crocodiles or pigs or something."

"Now you're talking," I grin at Roman. His idea sounds like a few hours of fun, and retribution for our Angel is my idea of a good time. Plus, I really don't want to kill her and won't on purpose if I don't absolutely need to. "I do enjoy a good flaying, and I have all the tools to make it perfect."

My mind flashes back to the last time I carefully peeled the skin from a piece of shit who was abusing women on the island. It was a pro bono job, and I enjoyed every moment of it. I can still hear his screams as I used a scalpel to detach his flesh from his muscle, to pull it apart from his ligaments and stretch it out on a clothes-drying rack while he watched in horror. It helps that I recorded the experience, and play it back now and then, reliving it. Having that memento keeps me refreshed and focused, and reminds me of what truly brings me joy.

"This sounds overly complicated with lots of risks involved," Slade snarls at Roman. "I think you just want to keep her here so you can put your dick inside her."

"Fuck you, Slade," Roman frowns and raises his voice. "Of

course, I wouldn't be opposed to doing that, but it's not why she's here."

"Why is she here then, man? Why is she still alive, creating all sorts of problems that we don't really need right now? It seems like incredibly poor decision-making by all involved." He glares at Roman and then at Aidan who officially 'signed off' on her being here. "I'm honestly shocked by how blasé you're being about this, Aidan, considering the damage she's already doing."

"Listen, I didn't mean to bring her into our bullshit, you know?" shrugs Roman. "She was an innocent bystander. And I still think she could be useful to us somehow."

We all turn to look at Aidan because he hasn't shared his plan yet. Of course, we all know he's going to make a reasonable suggestion, something less polarizing than what Slade and Roman have suggested.

I'm guessing he'll probably say that we should just leave her on the streets and be done with her. Put her out on the side of the road somewhere and tell her never to come back. Let the psycho come after her, and she can fend for herself.

That she's not our problem.

That she's ridiculously pretty, but that's not reason enough to compromise all of us and everything we've worked so hard for.

Putting her on the street makes more sense than putting us at risk.

He hates risk.

Imaginary Aidan is on a roll in my mind, pointing out all the reasons why it's bad for her to stay here and why the right thing to do is to kick her out immediately.

But the actual Aidan takes a deep breath and presses his lips together in a grimace. "I know I was against her coming here in the first place, but I think we have to let her stay."

I do a double-take because it seems like Aidan might be malfunctioning.

"Um, what? Did I mishear you?" Slade's jaw practically

unhinges as he raises an eyebrow, clearly also confused. "I thought you agreed on the risk she poses to us."

"No, you didn't mishear me," says Aidan, shaking his head. "She does pose a risk, you're right. I've agreed with that from the start and I still stand by that. But, like Roman said, she didn't start this. She didn't insert herself into our lives. We came flying into hers with murder and carnage and kidnapping. And now it turns out she has a psychopath who's followed her all the way here and is trying to hunt her down. We've inadvertently saved her once, twice even depending on how you think about it, and now I think we need to save her intentionally."

"Why? Because it's the 'good' or 'right' thing to do? Since when did we have a moral code? I thought the whole point was that we didn't." Slade crosses his arms over his chest. "Are you going soft on us now, after years of drumming it into our brains that we didn't come equipped with the misplaced sense of right and wrong that is the main downfall of our greatest rivals? Of reminding us that we should do what serves us, no matter what the implications are for other people? Brotherhood first and all that? Don't tell me you're changing your words to live by now over a piece of ass."

"We still don't have a moral code, Slade. Don't get things twisted. But, like I said, it's not her fault that Roman here went and murdered someone in her workplace. Or that we brought her here." He rubs at his bottom lip with his finger, a pensive expression on his face. "And we can hardly send her back to the salon or her apartment with this lunatic ready to skin her alive and wear her as a suit."

"But she's a risk. You hate risk," I peer at Aidan as I speak up.

He visually appears normal even though he might not sound like it right now. His pupils seem okay. His speech is clear. He doesn't appear to be under the influence of anything.

For once, I agree with Slade about something. Aidan saying Angel should stay with us is such a weird suggestion by him. All he does is talk about risk this, risk that, and now he's suddenly changing his tune.

I'm not sure what his deal is today, but his risk tolerance has apparently just skyrocketed to new heights. For Angel. Like being around her is shifting our DNA or something.

And Aidan doesn't just change like that. At least, he hasn't before.

Maybe Slade is right. Maybe she is weakening us from the center out.

"Sounds like someone's growing soft, forgetting where they came from and what they're all about," growls Slade, his eyes narrowing at Aidan. "I knew she would weaken us. Roman might think with his dick," he glares at Roman, "but I didn't expect you to be the one to fold so quickly, Aidan."

"Fucking chill out, Slade. Clearly, you disagree with me, but I'm not changing my mind. Having her here is the best thing for us collectively. It's what we need to do, so get on board, man." Aidan rarely makes threats, and I'm not sure quite what he's inferring will happen if Slade chooses not to.

"I didn't realize this was a dictatorship." The cords on Slade's neck are pulled taut and his face growing red, his pulse visible in his temples as he clenches his jaw.

He narrows his eyes at Aidan and shifts forward as if he's about to stand, and for a moment I think he's going to take a swing at him.

Aidan meets his glare, not backing down.

"Guys, stop it," I say. "All I care about is that we get to keep the girl. Angel can stay in my room if she wants protection," I add.

The other guys all turn and glare at me, momentarily distracted by my suggestion and slight change of subject.

"What?" I shrug. "Just making the offer."

Roman rolls his eyes. "Whatever, man. Anyway, I'm glad you have a reasonable perspective on this, as usual, Aidan. Even if not all of us can comprehend your wisdom right now." He narrows his eyes at Slade. "And I get to tell her about this, seeing I found her."

His demeanor changes at the mention of getting to speak with her. He beams at the prospect of saving his damsel in distress, of sharing the news that she gets to stay and that we'll do everything in our power to protect her.

"Hoping she'll run to you and put her arms around you and suck your dick because you're the one that told her?" I ask.

Roman juts his chin out at me, knowing it's the truth. "You're just jealous. You want to tell her so she'll suck *your* dick."

"Maybe," I say, crossing my arms over my chest.

Of course, I want to be the one that tells her she gets to stay with us, and that we're going to protect her. Because I want to see her smile. Because I want to be the reason that she smiles. A little bit of dick-sucking wouldn't go astray, either, but that's not expected.

There's something about this woman. I just want to make her happy, no matter what it takes.

"Listen, let's just give her a minute to settle. To process this information. I don't think anyone needs to run and tell her today," says Aidan. "Give her a while to cool down, maybe even a day or two."

"Won't she run if she thinks we don't want her here?" I ask. "What if she panics and finds a way to escape in the middle of the night because she's so afraid of what might happen to her here, of what we might decide? And then what if the psycho tracks her down and chops her to pieces, just because we didn't communicate right away?"

"Wow, you're really going on a mental journey there, Brick. To be honest, I think she's far more likely to run if she thinks we *do* want her here. She's spooked. She doesn't trust us yet, which is fair. Just give her some time and don't promise anything one way or another. Let her settle in a little."

Roman and I both glare at Aidan. He's always holding us back, trying to time things perfectly. Usually, he's right to do so.

He's the voice of reason in our chaos, and that's frustrating sometimes. Like now.

I sigh. "Fine, I won't say shit until you give the word. But I will be there for her if she wants to talk or just needs company in the meantime."

"So will I," nods Roman. "But I still get to tell her first when the time is right."

"Jesus, Roman. You're like a child. 'I get to tell her, I get to tell her first.'" I mimic him in a baby voice because that's what he fucking sounds like. Besides, I want to tell her and if she asks me I have every intention of doing so. Roman can fuck right off, he doesn't get special privileges just because he was the first one to lay eyes on her beautiful face.

"See? I told you this would happen," says Slade to Aidan, sighing heavily. "She's causing conflict between us. She's weakening our brotherhood. She's a massive distraction, even when she's on the other side of the house. She just might be the worst thing to ever happen to us."

CHAPTER 25

t's been a relatively quiet couple of days. The guys check in on me from time to time but mainly give me a wide berth. I think they're trying to be respectful and give me space after I shared what I did with them, but it's a bit lonely wandering around in this giant house by myself. I still don't have a phone, so I can't even scroll mindlessly through news feeds or play games while I watch reality shows.

I thought about cooking something, just for something to do to take my mind off things, but after taking a closer look at the kitchen and peeking in a few cupboards and drawers, I decide not to. Judging by how immaculate Slade keeps the kitchen, and how it seems to be his pride and joy, I assume any attempt to move things out of their correct positions would just turn into an argument. I'm really not in the mood for his judgmental looks and critical observations.

My mental and physical energy has been drained, and as I wander aimlessly from room to room, my limbs feel inexplicably heavy, like they're weighed down by my darkest thoughts. I feel like I'm sinking, like I'm drowning and I can't save myself. Nobody can save me now. I'm a dead woman walking.

Finally, I just give up and get onto my side on the couch in the living room and curl up into the fetal position while I watch more bad TV. It's not as much of a distraction as I need to truly take my mind off things, but it will have to do. It's the only option I have.

I'm a little out of sorts right now, and it's not just because I've found out my stalker is on the loose and trying to track me down and kill me. That's happened so often at this point I'm almost resigned to it as part of my life. The way some people learn to deal with chronic pain or an abusive parent, you just learn to endure it at the time and one day it becomes less noticeable, less intrusive on your everyday life. It's still terrifying but in a manageable way. I've gotten pretty good at compartmentalizing that type of stuff.

The thing I'm struggling with more, my acute issue, is what Roman has planned for this evening.

Because Roman is going on a date tonight.

It's with some woman he apparently met at one of the bars the guys own. He casually mentioned it earlier in the day, just brought it up in casual conversation, and it's all I've been able to think about ever since.

As he leaves to go and pick up his date, I feel a twinge in the pit of my stomach. I don't know why, though. It's not like I have any claim to him, or that I'd even want to claim him given the chance.

Hell, he's the one who came traipsing into my life and fucked it all up within less than an hour of being at the salon. He's the reason I'm here, kidnapped, captive in this house with these four men.

I should be furious with him, not pining over him because he's taking some woman out in the hopes she'll suck his dick at the end of the night.

Not that he needs to buy a woman a meal for her to be

begging to do that, I'm sure. I wish I hadn't trimmed his hair so neatly before The Asshole came in, and that I'd left it uneven and sticking up at weird angles. But even if his hair wasn't picture-perfect, I'm pretty sure he'd still have to beat women off with a stick. Damn Roman and his stupid hot face and murderous tendencies.

Realistically, it's just been a coincidence that not one of the guys has left my side, except to work, since I've been at the house. It was only a matter of time before they resumed everyday activities. They all probably regularly go on dates. For all I know, they might all have serious girlfriends.

Well, I take that back. When it comes to Roman, I doubt it, actually. He seems committed to non-commitment from what I've seen.

Many women would definitely try to ship Aidan, with his handsome looks, his muscular body, and his natural leadership qualities. He seems like a sexy but reliable choice. And with the whole belt incident I got the opportunity to see another side of him simmering just beneath the surface, one that I don't think many other people know exists. He's got that two-point-five-kids-white-picket-fence-potential vibe crossed with *Fifty Shades* meets *Sons of Anarchy*. And all of this makes him insanely hot.

Women probably go crazy over Brick for his wild unpredictability, his humor and his many quirks. He is fun and hot, a sexy and crazy ball of energy. I haven't seen his cock yet, but I already know it's huge. Brick has massive BDE.

I could see him pairing up with a cute vegan one day. They could wear matching faux leather jackets and spoon-feed each other quinoa in the park in the mornings, and torture evil people in the basement in the evenings. A match made in heaven.

And then there's Slade. He's probably best-suited to someone as cynical about life as him. A Pollyanna type would drive him nuts, and he definitely needs somebody with some depth.

Someone snarky and assertive who wouldn't put up with all his shit. Someone who gives back as good as he dishes it out. On second thought, that sounds way too much like me and it's obvious that we would be wildly incompatible. We're like oil and water.

Maybe what he really wants is someone who's sweet and submissive, who'll kiss the scowl right off his lips and whisper in his ear about how wonderful and special he is. Who'll cream herself when he cooks for her. Someone who will break down his walls layer by layer until he's actually capable of showing any feelings or engaging in a two-way conversation.

Maybe he deserves a bit of tenderness. Maybe that would mix with his own prickly personality and make him into a tolerable human being.

It's fun thinking about shipping the guys with imaginary women. But at the same time, the thought of it seems to have led to a burning sensation deep in my gut and my jaw is aching from me clenching it repeatedly.

Great, I'm getting jealous about imaginary scenarios that I'm creating in my mind. Jealous of the imaginary relationship lives of the *men who kidnapped me*. That's totally normal.

I guess it makes sense that I'm feeling this way. Despite the craziness of the circumstances, I've enjoyed how many things have been so far. I'm getting used to being around all four of the guys, and being the only female in this house.

Each of the guys has been attentive in his own way. Even if Slade's way is being an asshole. . He's lucky he's so sexy when he scowls. I feel a bit possessive of all of them, even though I haven't known them for long.

Even so, why am I so twisted up about Roman and this date?

Why do I care who he dates, or fucks, or whatever?

I've never been a jealous person, so why would I start now?

Still, I can't help but watch out the window as he leaves to go pick her up. He's dressed nicely, in one of his custom-tailored suits that fits him perfectly. Looking dashingly handsome as always.

He smelled good, too, as he walked out the door. The same

pomade I remember from the salon, cognac and tobacco, melding with an aftershave with notes of cedar wood and geranium. He seems to have a different scent for every occasion, so maybe this is his 'date a hottie and bang her brains out' fragrance of choice. I wanted to run over to him and bury my face in his neck and just inhale his deliciousness, but instead, I just sat there, frozen, as he left.

When he glanced at me on his way out the door, I almost melted onto the floor, but then I remembered he made himself look and smell this good for *her*, not for me. So, instead, I looked away and pretended not to be interested.

To make things worse, to make me really stew on things, he showed me a picture of his date earlier. She looked pretty in the photo, wearing a cute black dress, with a slim waist and perky tits, and her makeup and hair were done really nicely. Of course she's pretty. Roman can get any girl he wants. He probably doesn't have to slip below a ten... or maybe a nine on a rough day. I don't know why he showed the photo to me, but if it was to make me jealous, it worked.

I guess that's something a guy would do to a female friend, show them a picture of their date. Maybe that's why he hasn't tried to fuck me yet. He doesn't see me that way. I've heard of being friend-zoned, but being kidnapped and friend-zoned is new territory. I guess it could happen. Anything is possible.

Conjured images of them making out flood my mind. A montage of their hands and mouths and fingers and bodies mashing against each other.

I imagine them at a fancy restaurant, his hand sliding into her panties under the table while she smiles at him and pretends his fingers aren't buried deep inside her while she subtly bucks against his touch.

I imagine her stroking his hard shaft while he devours a steak, his precum leaking onto the leather booth and leaving his mark.

I imagine him bending her over the dining table and

ramming himself deep inside her cunt as the entire restaurant watches and applauds while he rails her, plates and glasses flying off the table and clattering to the ground, smashing everywhere as they orgasm together.

These scenarios are where my warped mind is taking me, and my heartburn is getting worse.

I exhale deeply and realize I've been gritting and grinding my teeth ever since I watched them leave, glaring out the window and waiting for his return so I can berate him like a jealous shrew. My jaw is clenched so tightly that one of my teeth does a weird thing, moving in a direction it's not meant to or something. I take a deep breath and consciously try to relax my body.

What is wrong with me? He's just a guy. A guy that would never be satisfied with just one woman, at that. From the moment I saw him, I knew he was a player. Dashing and charismatic and ready for the smooth lines to spin off his tongue like silk. So it shouldn't be a surprise that he's going on a date. That he's going to do what he was made to do, charm women and then fuck them senseless.

It doesn't stop me from being incredibly frustrated.

It's difficult to concentrate for the next few hours.

In an effort to make time go by faster, I mindlessly click between TV channels, scrolling through screen after screen of infomercials. Skincare products, exercise equipment, signal-blocking wallets, debt consolidation, ambulance-chasing lawyers. All of the jingles and accusations and authoritative tones melding into a swirl in my brain, making me want to scream. Finally, I change the channel to a reality TV marathon. People are screaming at each other but in a way that I can tune out. It helps that I've seen this episode before.

I try sitting on the couch, lying on my back, then my side, with and without a cushion. Nothing is comfortable right now. I can't relax. My body is tense.

I know I should go to my room and sleep, both because I'm

exhausted and because staying up and waiting for Roman is pointless. No good can come of it.

There's a saying that people shouldn't stay out all night, that if you go out you should get yourself home at a decent hour because nothing good happens after midnight. Well, I'm guessing that nothing good happens after hours of waiting for a fuck boy to get home after a date with a woman that's not you.

Despite my better judgement, despite knowing that I'm probably only going to get myself into more of a state as time ticks by, I find myself edging along the couch until I'm as close as possible to the front door so I there's no chance I'll miss him when he comes in.

Finally, after what seems like many hours, I hear the front door open, followed by Roman's deep voice and then the tinkling laugh of a woman. I glance toward the front door, and of course, the laugh is attached to the pretty woman he showed me a photo of earlier.

They're too distracted to notice me all the way over in the living room. Plus, they're probably not assuming someone would be up this late waiting to observe them when they come in.

He has his arm around her and they're both giddy, laughing about some secret joke they have between them. She looks to be as pretty in real life as she is in her pictures, all smiles and sparkling eyes and full lips that Roman keeps looking at like he wants to kiss and lick and bite.

She's touching his arm, clearly comfortable around him. Comfortable touching him. I wish I was touching him. She doesn't need to be here, in this house. I'm enough for Roman. He doesn't need her.

He only needs me.

But he refuses to have me.

Roman's body language noticeably adjusts, and I recognize it immediately. He's going in for the kill. I can see the hunger in his eyes as they roam over her body, making my stomach churn and my chest burn.

But I also feel a twinge between my legs at the intensity of the look he's giving her. His eyes are dark pinpoints, and they're smoldering. He emanates pure, hot lust like he wants to devour her completely. Like nobody else is in the universe, let alone the room.

Given the way he's visually feasting on her, there's little risk of him glancing over and seeing me. If he did happen to look over, I don't think he'd even notice I'm here. Everything seems to be invisible to him right now, except for her.

Who doesn't want to be looked at in that way by someone they're attracted to? Like you're the most delicious, amazing thing they've ever seen and they can't get enough of you? Like all they want to do is rip your clothes off and devour every part of you?

They walk through the dining area and head up the stairs, his arm wrapped around her waist, and they disappear into his room. The pit in my stomach multiplies, sending acidic ribbons up my esophagus.

I sit for a moment, unmoving, not sure what to do. But I can't just stay here.

Making sure to be very quiet, I head through the kitchen area and up the stairs, and tiptoe along the hallway. A trail of women's perfume, not mine, marks the path. Definitely not something I would wear. But maybe something he prefers. I'm learning all sorts of things about Roman today.

I'm slightly relieved to see his bedroom door is open a crack, because I don't know what I would have done if it was closed. I'm not sure if I could have handled not knowing what was going in there between Roman and *her*. I walk a little further down the hall and peek through the gap from a distance.

They haven't wasted any time. Roman is standing up and his date is on her knees in front of him. She reaches up to unbuckle his belt and he lets her. She slides it out of his belt loops and places it to the side.

He's facing the door, so he sees me watching almost immediately, and he smirks as his gaze settles on me. He continues watching me as she undoes his pants and frees his erection. He's hard as iron, his impressive cock ready to be inside her. Or inside me, but she'll have to do for now.

She grasps him in her palm and takes his cock between her plump lips. I stand there, watching, as she uses her hand to milk his shaft while she slides his cock down her throat, gliding it in and out of her red-rimmed mouth. She fondles his balls with her other hand and I almost want to call out 'good girl' because she's trying so hard to please him.

His eyes locked on mine, he grips the back of her head so he can fuck her mouth, and begins to roll his hips so that she has to take his cock at his pace. She gags briefly at the change of intensity but soon gets right back to it.

I can see her lipsticked lips and her tongue as they caress his hardness, and my pussy clenches at the thought of my own lips and tongue and hands being on him.

He closes his eyes for a moment as he shoves his cock down her throat and holds it there, her throat impaled by his hardness. His eyes flick open toward me as he continues to hold her mouth on him, his entire cock sitting down her throat. Her body stills, and she has no choice but to just stay there, unmoving, while he drains her of her air supply.

After several seconds, he gently lets her mouth off of his cock.

She pulls back and gasps for air, saliva dripping from his cock and her mouth onto the floor. She glances to the side briefly and her eyes are watering.

He helps her up and guides her around to the side of the bed and pushes her onto her back so she lays across the width of the mattress, her head closest to me, and he kisses her on the mouth.

Her arm wraps around his neck, pulling him to her. I see his tongue swipe through her lips, meeting with hers.

He looks up at me, his head above her field of vision, and he winks at me. I realize that he's had her lie at this angle so he can continue to make eye contact with me while they fuck.

His hand trails down the side of one of her breasts, along the orb-like curve, and she moans at his touch as he pulls her dress down to fully expose her chest. He cups one of her breasts with his hand and she moans, arching her back toward him.

Her nipples are hard, and he glances down and dips his head toward one of them. He kisses it and then looks back up at me. A small smirk forms on his lips.

He dips his head again, gently tugging on her nipple with his teeth this time, causing her to moan loudly. His eyes are locked on me as he twirls his tongue around her pebbled nipple and she arches her back.

He leans down and bites it, grazing it between his teeth, and she cries out as he clamps down on it, harder this time judging by her agitated cries.

He turns her around so that her head is toward the foot of the bed, her face out of my sight because of the angle of the door. I can still see all of him though, as well as her body from the shoulders down, but now I can see the entire length of his erect cock from the side. He trails his hand down her dress and hikes it up so that it's over her hips, exposing her panties, her feet flat on the bed, and her knees in the air.

Hooking his finger inside the thin material, he moves her panties to the side and rubs at her glistening slit. My pussy clenches as I watch his fingers slide into her. As he glides them in and out of her, I can hear that she's soaking wet, the slick coating glazing his fingers.

I imagine what his long fingers feel like, how they expertly caress and flick and rub in all the right places. I wonder how his cock feels when it's this hard, when he's this aroused. As if it's my throbbing pussy that he's about to pound himself into. Not this stupid bitch, whoever she is.

Anyway, what do I care? I'm not sure why I'm feeling so territorial, or why I'm watching him fuck her.

I haven't even kissed the guy.

He's clearly into this woman, he clearly wants nothing more than to spend the night railing her.

I guess it doesn't mean I can't watch, though. Because whether I'm jealous or not, watching this is hot.

I cup one of my breasts in my hand and begin to play with my nipple through my shirt, and I bite my lip while he watches my fingers.

My other hand slides down over my shorts and I begin to rub myself through my pants and let out a silent moan. I slide my hand inside my panties, trailing a finger down my slit. I'm even wetter than I realized.

He climbs over her, mounting her, while his eyes stay locked with mine. My pussy clenches as he reaches down to line his rock-hard cock up with her entrance.

Eyes still on me, he glides into her with one thrust and she cries out his name. I feel my arousal begin to pool as I watch him bury himself inside her wet cunt. I'm craving him, I want so badly for him to be inside me instead. It should be my pussy that he's buried deep inside, not hers.

She cries out, louder now, as he begins to slam into her with increased force. There's no gentleness, just raw lust, as he begins impaling her on his cock.

I watch as he rhythmically grinds his hips against her, sinking himself deep into her wet cunt and pulling his cock slowly back out almost all the way, only to slam it in again even harder each time.

I like the way his strong hands grab her hips so tightly that she can barely move, controlling her so that his cock can take her exactly how it wants. She'll almost definitely have bruises in the morning.

I feel a twinge between my legs at the thought of him holding me like that and marking me, giving me something to remember him by that would last for days. I want him to cover me in bruises that remind me of him and our sex every time I look in the mirror.

Spreading my legs further apart as I stand there, my fingers skim over my clit and down to my entrance to collect some of my arousal. I gently roll my hips in rhythm with his thrusting as I work my fingers over my clit, letting out another silent moan at how good it feels to touch myself with his eyes on me.

He bites his lower lip as his gaze drops to my fingers as I work myself over, and his thrusts intensify.

His date's tits bounce around as he holds her hips steady, rolling his own so that he slides almost all the way out and then slams in again, hard, burying his cock completely inside her. I flick my clit faster to match his pace with my fingers.

It's like he's using her body for my benefit. She's just a vessel that he's working over to demonstrate what he wants to do to me. I feel pity for her, not having any idea that he's using her body to fuck my mind.

I feel someone press up behind me and nip me on my neck.

Startled, I pause my fingers.

"Want some help, Angel?" a voice whispers from behind me.

It's Aidan.

I turn my head to face him, and he leans down and kisses me, his tongue sliding into my mouth and searching for mine.

He reaches around and his hand joins mine inside my panties, and he silently groans as he feels how wet I am.

"Jesus, Angel," he whispers, as he begins to massage my clit with his finger. "You're dripping. Are you enjoying watching Roman fuck his date?"

He bites on his lower lip and I can feel a bulge in his pants as he presses his body into my back.

I nod.

"You're a naughty girl, watching them fuck," he whispers. "I like it."

I continue to roll my hips in time with Roman's cock thrusting into his date's pussy, Aidan's fingers rubbing my clit in rhythm. I grind my ass into him and he occasionally slides one or two long fingers inside me and then returns to focus his attention on my clit.

Roman's eyes are still locked on me, but his gaze has lowered and is now fixated on Aidan's fingers working over my clit.

Roman begins to thrust faster as he watches Aidan finger-fucking me, his cock slamming forcefully into his date, and Aidan matches his pace with his fingers.

I moan and he presses his body against me from behind. I can feel his hardness, his erection pressing firmly into my back as he unravels me with his fingers.

Biting his lower lip as he watches me, Roman reaches down with one of his hands and begins to stroke his date's clit.

She moans and begins to rock and grind her hips to get more traction against his hand.

"You're close now, baby, aren't you? I can tell," he growls, and she replies that she is but his eyes are looking at me when he speaks. "I want you to come all over my cock," he grinds out, his eyes still locked on me. "I want to hear you scream my name while I bury myself deep inside your sweet cunt."

Her body tenses, and she screams his name as she comes, arching her back and writhing on his cock.

Aidan presses on my clit with extra pressure, pinching it, sending me over the edge as well, my knees buckling and almost giving out underneath me.

My eyes roll back but then flick straight to Roman, and seeing me come sends him over the edge as well. His body stutters as he expels his release, and he buries himself to his hilt, his head tilting back as he groans.

She moans loudly, having no idea what's going on beside her.

Poor, naïve woman. He just came for me. It was seeing me come that took him over the edge. She may as well not even have been there.

He slowly slides himself out of her and snaps off his condom, discarding it on the nightstand.

Aidan pulls his hands out of my pants and nips me on my neck again. I grin and squeal. Roman's date glances over at the noise and she sees us standing at the doorway, Aidan removing his hand from my panties.

We shrug and grin, and I grab Aidan's hand as we run up the hallway laughing.

This was just the distraction I needed.

———

Done with spying on Roman and his date, I clean up and head back to the living room. When I walk down the hallway past Roman's room I don't look in. I don't need to see the aftermath of what just happened in there.

If I'm honest, I don't want to see them snuggling or having gentle post-coital moments together. It's one thing to watch him plow his cock into her like she was just a hole, but anything intimate would send me over the edge, and not in a good way.

I'm kind of hoping that seeing Aidan and me standing there watching was enough to start a fight between them, to piss the woman off so she just leaves. There's nothing I'd rather see right now than her running out of his room and out the front door in hysterical tears. I don't like her being here at all. I feel territorial, having another woman here rubs me the wrong way. But I haven't heard any raised voices or yelling, so I'm not sure how he explained away our being there. Some clever fuck boy excuse, most likely.

As these cluttered thoughts rush through my brain, I try to analyze them clinically.

I'm quite aware that I'm being ridiculous.

I've known these guys for a couple of days and they took me against my will.

It's not like I'm the queen of their fucking family who has any say in how they live their lives. I've barely been let out of a locked room, for goodness' sake.

My interest in the sex lives of my captors is probably far from healthy.

I really need to chill.

I take a seat on the couch. It's late, but Brick and Slade just got back from a job and Aidan obviously just got done finger-fucking me, so we're all awake. They're all night owls, anyway, I've found.

They're half-watching some show on TV and chatting about business. I pay partial attention to what they're saying, but the rest of me is focused on any sounds or signs of life coming from Roman's room.

I need his date to be over, and then I'll hopefully be able to relax.

Finally, his date leaves, her hair still tousled from being dicked down by Roman. She glances at us awkwardly, putting her hand up in a half-wave as she hurries past the living room, and he sees her out the front door.

Thank goodness he didn't let her stay the night. That would have ruined me.

As he turns away from the entrance, he turns toward the living room and sees me there observing him with the rest of the guys.

He walks over and sits on the armchair opposite the couch.

He nods in greeting to each of the other guys, then his gaze meets mine and he smirks.

I roll my eyes at him, but feel a flush creeping up my neck and spreading across my cheeks, exposing me.

"I learned something interesting today," he says to the other guys. "Angel, as it turns out, is a bit of a voyeur. Got off watching me burying my cock inside my hot date."

He winks at me, and I narrow my eyes at him.

"Like you can talk," smirks Brick. "You like to watch, too, Roman. I can't count the number of times we've been fucking someone and have looked over and you were there."

Roman shrugs.

Brick laughs. "And remember when you tried that free trial of the porn subscription and then it kept auto-renewing and so you kept it streaming 24/7 for a while?"

Slade snorts. "That was a moment to remember, for sure."

"That's all fair," Roman shrugs and grins, and then looks over at Aidan. "And I already knew you were a voyeur, bro."

He laughs in Aidan's direction, and Aidan shrugs as well. "It would have been rude not to join in with Angel here. She was having fun by herself, but I wanted to help her." He turns to me and winks. "Not that it looked like you needed any help."

"Thanks for your assistance," I snort. My pussy clenches as I think about the way his fingers felt as he caressed me. It was like he knew exactly how I like to be touched.

And having Roman's eyes locked onto mine as he buried himself in someone else… it was sensory overload, sending me over the edge as I watched his engorged cock slam in and out of her. Making me come apart without even touching me. But only because the whole time I was imagining she was me, that I was her.

Making me want Roman, more than ever, to give me the one thing he's refused to do so far.

It's another distraction from my pain. I want to be railed by Roman. I want him to control my body and do whatever he wants with it. But first, I need to figure out why he won't.

———

After chatting about business for a while more, Aidan, Brick and Slade leave the living room and head off in separate directions.

As usual, Aidan has work to do and retreats to his study, Slade heads to the kitchen, and Brick heads downstairs to his basement. From some unusual noises I heard when he and Slade returned from their job, I'm fairly certain they didn't come home alone and Brick is about to have a long night doing what he loves.

I linger behind, standing near the entrance to the living room while Roman absentmindedly flicks through channels on the TV.

I need to speak with him about what happened earlier. About everything.

He raises an eyebrow at me when he sees me just standing there, looking at him.

"You left the door open on purpose, didn't you?" I say, meeting his gaze. "You wanted me to watch you fuck her."

"Maybe." He smirks at me and shrugs.

"Why? Were you trying to make me jealous?"

He peers at me through his eyelashes, a small smile on his lips. "Did it work?"

"No. Saved me the time of fucking you after I saw your technique. You're like a fucking woodpecker with your cock. The least sexy fuck boy I've ever seen in the sack."

He smirks because I'm being ridiculous and he's a cocky asshole. He knows he's amazing in bed and his cock is nothing to be ashamed of.

That's why he carries himself so confidently, like the way he just strolled into my salon the other day acting like he owned the place.

"I think you're lying. I saw the way you watched, you couldn't get enough. If I really looked like a woodpecker while I fucked, that would mean you had some weird woodpecker fetish, the way you were rubbing your fingers all over your clit, matching the pace of my thrusts. The way you came all over Aidan's hand while you watched me burying my cock inside my date. You don't fool me with your insults, Angel. You wanted to be her."

My pussy clenches again. "I was just horny, I guess." I shrug. "It was just like watching porn. It did the job but I've seen much better. It would be a mistake if you thought it was anything more than that."

He smirks at me again, as if he sees right through me.

"Oh really?" He raises an eyebrow. "Do go on. Is there any other commentary you'd like to provide regarding my sexual prowess?"

"Yeah, actually, there is. Next time you fuck someone, you should really make eye contact with them. Instead of staring at another person standing in your doorway. It seems like maybe you wished you were fucking someone else, not the person you had your cock buried in."

In reality, watching him fuck his date was an intense experience and one I don't care to repeat again.

I saw the way he used his hips to rhythmically thrust into her, and the way her body responded to his touch. I saw the way he used his forearms and strong legs to dominate her, to position her body how he saw fit, to get at all the angles that brought him the most pleasure and delivered him exactly what he needed.

I saw the way he used her body while his gaze was locked with mine.

He was rough but intentional, controlling but sensual. Doing enough to make her think he was into her, but reserving his eye contact for me. Being sent over the edge only when he saw me come apart.

I want to see him do all those things again, but only if he's doing them to me.

Just thinking about it makes my pussy throb. I want him so badly.

As skilled as Aidan was with his fingers, I'm craving what Roman gave to his date tonight.

I need him inside me, and I won't give up until I get it.

As for any more bitches coming around, as far as I'm concerned, there will be no more dates.

I'm staking a claim to Roman.

He's mine now. They all are.

They just don't know it yet.

CHAPTER 26

ANGEL

"We've come to a decision," says Aidan.

I've been summoned to the living room once again.

His tone is serious, and I can't quite pinpoint the expression in his eyes. He always looks a little serious and tense, even when he's being playful. And definitely when he's whipping my ass with a leather belt to teach me a lesson. Right now's no different… there's no amusement, but he doesn't look angry or sad. I'm usually good at reading people, but he makes it difficult, like he's in advanced mode when it comes to accurately interpreting his emotions.

The guys are once again perched on the couch and armchair. I'm sitting on the very end of the couch facing them. All eight eyes are on me.

After the whole Roman date debacle, I spent last night tossing and turning. Every time I'd fall asleep, I'd bolt back upright as nightmares and memories collided, full of stalkers and torture and evil. It was hard to differentiate real memories from my imagination, but all of it was terrifying.

So I'm feeling pretty groggy and disoriented, my brain fuzzy from lack of sleep and the residual emotional overload that comes from a realistic, traumatic nightmare.

Roman just came to collect me from my room and said they had something to tell me. I have no idea what it's about, but if I had to guess it has something to do with my future with them. It's the only decision I can think they'd take the time to announce to me.

"I'm going to need a coffee for this," I say, as a headache starts to form at the base of my skull. I don't actually expect anyone to get up and get me a coffee, but Brick bolts from his seat and comes back a couple of minutes later with an espresso in hand.

"Coffee for the pretty lady," he says, smiling and handing it to me.

"Thanks, Brick," I say, taking the piping hot espresso cup from him and inhaling a deep sip, enjoying the warming sensation as the smooth brown liquid runs down my throat and gives me life.

I turn to Aidan. "So, you were saying?"

"Great, now that the princess is partially caffeinated, I'll continue," he smirks. "I was saying we've come to a decision."

"Oh good. You've decided to kill me? Please get it over with so I can be at peace." I put my hands up in a praying motion. I half mean it.

"Two of us suggested that, but we were overruled," scowls Slade.

"Oh you did, did you? You really hate me that much?" I glare at him. I genuinely don't know why he hates me so much that he wishes me dead.

"It's nothing personal," he shrugs. "I just see you as an obstacle to our success, and part of my job is to make sure those types of obstacles are removed. Do I feel bad you're in this situation through no fault of your own? Of course. Does that change how I feel about it, in terms of the best course of action? No."

"You're a fucking charmer, aren't you, Slade?" I narrow my eyes at him. "So you're saying two people overruled two people? Not sure how that math works, but okay," I roll my eyes. "You could have had me be the tiebreaker and got your wish. And who was the other person who thought killing me was a good idea?" I glance around the room as if I'm being hunted, trying to figure out the second predator.

My eyes settle on Aidan, but I doubt it would be him, although he might see disposing of me as a form of risk mitigation given I observed one of his brothers kill someone. That said, he tends to have the final say on nearly every decision here, so I'm assuming he has something to do with the whole killing me plan being overruled. I'll keep him on the 'maybe' list for now.

I glance at Roman next, and his eyes meet mine. They're pleading with me, trying to convey an invisible message. I know he's a charming ladies' man and can put on an act when he wants to, but I can't imagine him wanting to kill me. At least not until after he fucks me. But then he also doesn't want to fuck me. Jesus, these guys are confusing.

Then I look at Brick. He looks away. "Brick!" I cry out, my voice wavering and tears threatening to fill my eyes. "Brick, did you say you vote to kill me?" This one really stings. I was beginning to think he cared about me.

"I don't want you to die, Angel," he says, his voice low. "I just said that if you did have to die, that I would rather do it myself so that it was quick and you felt no pain."

"You'd kill me?" My eyes bore into his. I want to know exactly where I stand with this man, and whether I can trust him.

"In the sweetest way," he says, shrugging.

"That's… cute, I guess?" I've never been more conflicted about someone's desire to end my life, but because it's Brick, I decide to give him a pass for now.

I glance around at the rest of them. "So, given this vote was overruled, I'm assuming a decision was made not to kill me immediately. That's nice. Was there anything else to this decision?"

"There was more," says Roman. "We want you to stay with us."

"You what? Stay with you?" I look around at all four of them in an effort to better understand what Roman just said. "What do you mean?"

"We want to protect you. You stay here and we'll take care of you," says Brick, smiling at me. "We'll make sure that nobody ever hurts you again."

"Oh really, how ironic," I glance at Aidan and he smirks. He glances at my ass. He knows exactly what I'm talking about.

"Except for us, to clarify," he says, and Brick nods in agreement. "We get to hurt you. But only if you want us to, only the good pain."

Brick nods some more. "Lots of good pain."

"Even if it attracts a homicidal lunatic to your doorstep?" I raise an eyebrow.

I don't think they realize the lengths my stalker will go to in order to get to me. These guys are strong and can take care of themselves, but I also doubt they've come across anyone like him before.

He's not a simple drug dealer or a thief or a human trafficker that has his eye on something logical like money or power.

He's a stone-cold killer, and he is fixated on destroying everything and everyone I care about before ending my life in a torturous grand finale. He can't be reasoned with, because there's nothing else he wants. There's no logic with him, just a deadly obsession.

If… when… he finds out that I'm here, all four of these men are going to be added to the list of people he'll use to get to me.

Brick grins and his eyes glimmer with cruel excitement. "Even better. I have a feeling he's going to be spending some time in my basement soon. I can't wait!"

"Are you planning on making me stay in my room again

while I'm here? I know I was only meant to be out for a while, but I also didn't anticipate this being an ongoing situation." I raise an eyebrow. I have no desire to be locked in there all day, every day.

"No, you're one of us now," says Aidan. "You'll be free for the most part."

Slade chokes and starts to cough. It seems this part of the decision has taken him by surprise. "She's not one of us," he mutters under his breath, "and she never will be."

Aidan glares at him but doesn't speak further.

This is a lot of information to process. A moment ago these guys were my kidnappers, and I was their captive. Technically still I am. But now they're wanting to keep me here on a longer-term basis, with more freedom.

I don't have many options, really, when I think about it. No family or friends here. Nobody I really know.

Except for a psycho who's trying to hunt me down and kill me and doing one hell of a good job of the first part.

I'm clearly not going to show up on his doorstep, wherever that is, asking for a place to stay.

"Why are you being so kind to me?" I glance around the room, making eye contact with each of them one by one.

Slade looks away.

"Most of you, at least," I add.

"Listen, it's my fault you're here in the first place," says Roman. He looks at the ground as if he's ashamed to have put me in the worst situation of my life.

A weird thought occurs to me, and I snort involuntarily.

My snort is followed by a laugh that starts small but quickly builds into an uncontrollable belly laugh.

My entire body shakes as I cackle, my abs shrieking at me as my stomach clenches into itself with my unabashed laughter. This probably makes me seem like an absolute lunatic, but I just can't stop.

The guys all peer at me as if I've lost my mind.

"What?" asks Roman, squinting at me. "What's going on with you? Did we do some damage when we hit you in the head?"

That only serves to make me laugh even more.

"Jesus, we've permanently damaged her," Slade shakes his head.

I take giant gulps of air and put my hand on my chest in an effort to calm myself. Finally, my hysterics peter out to a giggle and I regain my composure.

"It's just that…" I resist the urge to start laughing again, pressing my lips together firmly to keep it all in, "ironically, I think you might have just saved my life, all four of you. Especially you, Roman. Fuck me, what a twist!"

"How so?" Roman arches an eyebrow.

"Well where do you think I would have been when… *he*… came after me if you hadn't brought me here?" I put my hands up in an exaggerated shrug.

The guys glance at each other, realization dawning in their eyes.

"Exactly. Either at work or at home. Two of the only places you'll ever find me. And there would have been a near one hundred percent chance I'd have been by myself."

I pause and nod at them.

"Yep, that's right. I can see you're getting it. He went to the only places I really go. In which case, I would almost certainly not be alive anymore. By committing a murder in front of my face, causing you to kidnap me… Roman, you saved my life!"

Roman's eyes grow large, and then he narrows them and smirks. "So… what you're saying, Angel… is that you owe me, big time?" He winks at me and grins. "Sounds like it might be time to pay up."

Without thinking, I jump up and race over to him, and plant a giant kiss straight on his lips.

He pulls me closer to him and kisses me back, hard, and I

know my lips are going to bruise. But I don't care and in fact I kind of like it.

I close my eyes and tilt my head back and run one of my hands through his hair as our lips stay connected. He grabs me with one hand by the back of my neck, controlling the angle of my head, tilting it up to meet his.

The kiss turns passionate, and I moan softly as his tongue swipes through my lips and entangles itself with my own. We wrestle, each of our tongues trying to gain control.

I feel a throb beginning in my core as he deepens the kiss, pushing his tongue further inside my mouth. I respond by sucking on his tongue with mine.

He groans, cupping my ass with the hand that's not holding my neck, and grinds his body against me, his erection poking me in the stomach.

My pussy is throbbing intensely now, wet heat forming inside me.

I really wouldn't be alive right now if it wasn't for him. For these guys. The thought is exhilarating, my body electric at the realization.

"Get a fucking room, guys," snarls Slade, wrenching me out of my little mental bubble that only contains kisses with Roman. Out of the corner of my eye I can see he's glaring at us, but he doesn't look away.

I keep kissing Roman and close my eyes again to block Slade out. To block everything else out except for Roman's lips and his tongue and his hands. My mind flashes back to watching him and his date fucking, but, in my imagination, it's me he's sinking his cock into. I much prefer it this way.

"You know what?" asks Roman, not expecting nor wanting an answer. "Maybe we will get a room."

He grabs my hand and intertwines my fingers with his. "We'll see you later, folks," he grins. "I have a damsel in distress to take care of. She owes me big time!"

I giggle as he pulls me towards the stairs and we bound up them together, racing toward his room as the others look on. I glance behind me and Slade is still scowling as he watches us leave.

Brick has a funny grin on his face, and although I'm far away now, I swear I see a bulge in his pants.

And Aidan looks conflicted, but doesn't say anything. He just watches us leave.

Oh well, not my problem. Roman just saved my life. It might be in one of the weirdest ways I could possibly think of, but it still counts.

And I intend to show him just how grateful I am.

CHAPTER 27

ROMAN

Well, that's one way of thinking about what transpired over the past few days. I'm a murderer and a kidnapper, and now I can add a goddamn superhero to my list.

I saved Angel's life.

Sure, it was unintended and entirely coincidental, but she seems keen on thanking me for my efforts, so who am I to stand in her way?

I knew this day would come when I could be with her, and that it wouldn't be far off. It's just a little sooner than I expected.

She's an amazing kisser. The way she ran her fingers through my hair, her tongue wrestling with mine, was so fucking sexy. I could feel the heat emanating from her body.

And when she sucked on my tongue with her own... Jesus. She clearly knows what to do with that thing. I can't wait to feel it wrapped around my cock.

By the time Slade yelled at us to get a room, I was rock hard, and I didn't need any encouragement to grab her hand and bound up the stairs towards my bedroom.

She seems giddy, laughing and smiling at me, but I also recognize the lust in her eyes. I guess it's that 'saved by a super-hero' afterglow that you see in action movies, where the hero saves the damsel in distress and she wants to give her body over to him immediately. Again, unexpected, but I'll take it.

This gorgeous woman is about to be mine, and I know all the guys are jealous, even Slade.

I open my bedroom door and tug her inside, not bothering to close it. I pull her to the bed and have her sit down next to me, and I turn to face her.

Our lips meet again, our kiss is more frantic this time.

I pull away, grabbing her ponytail and using it to yank her neck to the side so I can trail little butterfly kisses down her neck and over her throat.

I nip playfully at the side of her neck and she moans huskily, which only serves to make me even harder.

Using my other hand to cup her breast, I can feel through her thin top that her nipple is rock hard. Through the fabric, I roll it between my thumb and finger and she groans.

"Oh my god, Roman," she gasps, her breath struggling to keep up with the intensity of our kiss and my hands on her body.

I urgently need her breasts in my mouth, so I roughly yank her tank top down so it cups her tits from below. They're gorgeous, full orbs with rock-hard rosy nipples pointing at me, urging me to do bad things to them.

"Fuck, you have beautiful tits," I rasp, my breath coming heavy and hard.

Her body language suddenly changes, and she stills, her eyes meeting mine. The dark lust in her eyes has been replaced by something else. Her mouth is tight and her body looks tense.

"Do you really want to be doing this? Are you sure you don't want to just go on another date and bring them back here?" Her chin trembles slightly as she juts it out, perhaps a combination of anger and hurt. She bites her lip, but not in a seductive way. It's like she's clamping down on it with her teeth so that her eyes stop watering.

I dip my head and twirl my tongue around her nipple and she shudders, her jealous eyes clouding with lust. "Why? Are you jealous, Angel?"

"No, I've seen you fuck," she snaps. "I'm the opposite of jealous. I'm relieved." She frowns, but her voice is soft.

"Come on, now. You could see that I know what I'm doing." I try to tease her, gently.

"It seems like that performance was more for my benefit than yours."

"Maybe it was," I say, tugging her nipple gently with my teeth, causing her mouth to open in a quiet moan. "Maybe it was entirely for you. Did you enjoy it?"

Her face flushes, and she looks away.

CHAPTER 28

"You did. You enjoyed watching my cock slamming in and out of her, making her moan, didn't you? You enjoyed watching me make her come apart while you touched yourself, while Aidan worked you over with his fingers. While my eyes were on you."

My flush intensifies. My pussy is throbbing intensely from what his tongue has been doing to my nipple.

"It was only ever about you, Angel," he says softly.

He stands up, takes my hand and kisses it, and then guides me over to the full-length mirror at the end of the bed.

He stands behind me and I look down at the ground, but he grabs my chin and tilts my head so that I'm forced to look at myself.

I normally hate looking at myself in the mirror and try to avoid it for the most part, but seeing he's forcing me to look, I check out my reflection. My skin is a little flushed and I'm glowing.

"Look at you," he says, holding my chin in place. "You're beautiful," he whispers.

I cast my eyes down, avoiding my reflection again, looking anywhere but at the face that follows me everywhere I go.

"No, I'm serious. Don't look away. Look at yourself." He tilts my jaw up further. I sigh, shift uncomfortably, and then finally look in the mirror again. Properly this time.

My reflection stares back at me. I look okay, I guess. Maybe a little tired after waiting up for hours to monitor Roman and his date.

"You're fucking gorgeous. None of us can keep our hands off you. That woman I brought home was hot, but so what, big deal. There are lots of hot women around here. They're a dime a dozen, especially when the other guys and I look the way we do. Not to mention how women cream themselves when they realize we have power on this island, that we own bars and clubs and have a place in Tane's ranks. Their panties basically fall off when we walk past," he shrugs. He's a cocky asshole, but I have a feeling he's not exaggerating. "But you, Angel, are out of this fucking world. Off the planet. Exquisite. Nobody can hold a torch to you."

I don't know how to take his words. He's definitely a smooth talker, but as he holds my head in place, forcing me to see myself the way he sees me, his eyes remain locked on mine.

This doesn't seem like a line to get into my pants. I think he's pretty clear that I want him there, and he's the one playing hard-to-get for whatever reason. He could have just fucked me the moment we got into this room, but instead, he's taking the time to really make me look at myself, to make me understand how he and the others see me.

My body quivers as he keeps his eyes trained on mine, and, standing behind me, he lowers his hand inside my shorts until it rests on top of my thin sliver of underwear.

"I don't know why you bother wearing these around here, Angel," he growls in my ear. "There's really no point. You should just walk around naked all the time. None of us would complain."

My pussy clenches at the thought of never wearing any clothing in this house. Of wandering around stark naked, so that the guys have easy access to my breasts and everywhere else to touch and caress and pleasure at any moment.

"We'd need to put towels down everywhere. The four of you turn me into a perpetual puddle," I rasp, my voice husky at the visions of debauchery that play out in my mind.

He growls and sucks my earlobe into his mouth and drags his teeth over it, his cool breath making little goosebumps form on my neck.

He moves his hand up slightly and then slips it beneath my panties, touching my bare mound with his strong fingers and letting them rest there as we both watch in the reflection of the mirror.

"You're right, your pussy is soaking because you're so turned on. Do you like the way my fingers feel on your pussy, Angel? Are you craving more?"

I nod. It's as if he reads my mind. My pussy throbs at how close he is to touching me in my most sensitive places. I yearn for him, but he momentarily keeps his hand still.

"I enjoy having you around, Angel," he says, his voice husky.

I moan as he trails his fingers down over my clit and down over my slit, watching his fingers in the reflection as if he's touching someone else. But it's me this time. It's where he's meant to be.

"I can't stop thinking about how good you must taste. I'm constantly hard thinking about it. I dream about tasting your sweet cunt and letting it drip all over my face."

I grind back against him, feeling his hardness pressing into me. "Why don't you do something about that, then?" I ask, my eyes not leaving his. "Or why don't you let me take care of this?" I ask, reaching back and rubbing his rock-hard shaft.

"In good time, Angel," he rasps in my ear. "I'm going to dictate our pace. Be patient."

My breath grows ragged as he begins to stroke me, his

fingers languidly caressing my slit and occasionally causing shock waves as they feather across my clit.

He removes his other hand from my jaw and moves it to the back of my head, where he pulls my hair back in a ponytail and wraps it around his fist, exposing one side of my neck.

He kisses and nips at the curve of my neck and my shoulder, and I cry out as his teeth drag along my skin.

"Why don't you want to fuck me, Roman? I can't stop thinking about what your cock will feel like buried deep in my pussy."

I've never had to beg a man before, but Roman seems to be playing hard to get with his cock, despite being generous with his mouth and his hand.

His eyes remain locked on mine, and I tilt my head back, gasping for air as he continues to massage my clit with his fingers.

He looks at my exposed throat in the mirror again, then dips his head. I moan as I feel his mouth suctioning onto the skin on my neck. He's marking me, showing the world I belong to him.

"Roman," I moan as he collects more arousal from my entrance with his finger and swirls it around my clit.

Without a word, he pulls me away from the mirror and leads me to the bed.

CHAPTER 29

ROMAN

I continue my trail of kisses down her chest and onto one of her breasts, where I circle her nipple with my tongue, resuming where we left off before I guided her over to the mirror.

It was worth the pause. She needs to know how I see her, how we all see her. How much she means to us, and how she's so different from any other woman we've ever met.

It was a struggle to get her to look at herself, really see herself, but she seemed to enjoy watching my fingers working her over in the reflection.

She moans hungrily as I suck her nipple into my mouth, dragging my teeth gently along her delicate skin. Her nipple is rock hard and pebbled, and I let my tongue swirl around its perimeter, savoring the textured feeling on my tongue.

She digs her fingers into my back and arches her own so that her breasts press up toward me, showing me she wants more.

I suck harder and then apply more force with my teeth and she cries out, her nails digging harder into my back.

I groan, my cock throbbing with desire.

The effect this woman has on my body is electric. There are so many things I want to do to her it's making me crazy.

This is only the beginning.

I think about paying equal attention to her other nipple, but I'm hungry for her pussy and I'm ready to feast.

I look up at her for a moment and almost come in my pants at the look on her face. Her mouth is open slightly, her breath fast and audible. She's flushed with a light sheen on her skin as she gazes at me. I can tell she's wondering if I'm going to bury my cock in her today.

She's fucking phenomenal, and this is just the surface.

I pull her down the bed so her hips are right at the edge. I unbutton her shorts and slide them off as she watches me. Removing her panties, I spread her thighs apart and kneel in front of her pussy.

"Fuck, you're gorgeous," I say, marveling at her slick, pink folds. "And you're so fucking wet. Does it get you off when I save your life, baby?"

"Mmm, yes. Saving my life is hot," she says back, dreamily. "You're my superhero."

I kiss her on her pussy. "Good, me too. Protecting you makes me hungry as well."

She smiles, her eyes dark with desire, and I dip my head, licking and sucking and gliding my tongue up and down her slit like I haven't eaten in days.

"Fuck!" I gasp. "How do you taste so good?" I definitely haven't had anything nearly this sweet.

She gasps as I gently lap at her clit and then lick my way down to her entrance. I plunge my tongue inside, savoring her sweetness. She's sopping with arousal and I want to taste every last drop.

I feel her body shiver with pleasure as I drag my tongue back up her slit and circle her clit. I merge my own saliva with her wet heat, flattening my tongue against her clit and making a sticky mess that smears all over my mouth and between her thighs.

She's fucking delicious, and the messier the better. I'll never wash my face again. She tastes so fucking good.

I want her all over me. I could eat her out every day, and I'd still never be satisfied. It would never be enough.

"Mmm," she moans. "I thought *I* was supposed to be thanking *you*."

"Oh, believe me, you are. I was hungry, and this is just what I was craving. Tasting your dripping cunt is exactly what I want right now."

She moans, and I make eye contact with her as I continue to feast on her pussy, tilting her hips so that she can see my tongue lapping at her like a starved man.

I increase the pace of my licks, and she gasps, her hips bucking forcefully.

I can tell that she's getting close as she wraps her legs around my head, grabbing my hair in her fists and pulling my face closer into her cunt. I groan, enjoying the feeling of my face being mashed against her wetness as I continue to suck on her swollen bud.

Her thighs tremble, and then I feel her whole body tense. Her back arches and she cries out, her hips wildly thrashing against my face. Her fingers grab fistfuls of my hair, almost ripping out handfuls, and I couldn't care less. I would go bald voluntarily. I'd lose all my hair to worship this pussy every day for the rest of my life.

Jesus, one taste of this woman and my priorities have flipped on their head. Slade was right. She's dangerous.

I groan as she cries out, her voice husky with pleasure, and I continue to lick and suck at her clit. She's not getting away from my mouth just because she came apart once under my tongue. I have more I want to give her.

She squirms underneath me and pulls my hair tighter as I continue to lash her with my tongue. I feel a few hairs come loose as she wrenches them from the root while she bucks and writhes against my face, but I don't let her go.

The air in the room hangs thick with her arousal, and I can't get enough.

I continue to feast on her, to devour her core. Her body tenses back up as I bite down on her clit and she comes again, arousal dripping and smearing all over my face as she arches her back and writhes against me once more.

"Oh my fucking god, Roman!" she screams, panting, gasping for air. Her cries are loud, and I am enjoying every moment of this.

It only adds to it that the other guys probably can't avoid hearing it if they tried. They might even be watching through the door that I intentionally left ajar, but I don't look up to check. I'm too focused on her, on bringing her pleasure.

If I hadn't technically saved her, she wouldn't be here for me to treat like this. I don't want to think about what could have happened if I hadn't taken her from the salon. But I force the dark thoughts out of my mind for now. She's here right now, and that's what matters.

I continue licking and sucking on her engorged clit, and she cries out as I make her come again, shuddering against my face.

As her orgasm subsides, she collapses across the bed. Her legs stay spread apart as she lays there panting, spent. I look up at her and lick my lips as I regain my own breath, well aware the lower half of my face is completely covered in her arousal. Her own thighs are slick with my saliva and her own wetness, and they glisten in the near-darkness of my room, illuminated only by my alarm clock and the dim light from further down the hallway.

My cock is rock hard, and I'd love nothing more than to bury it deep inside her sweet, soaking cunt. I imagine that's what she's expecting, the way she's lying there, looking at me, begging me with her eyes to fill her up.

But I just can't right now. It doesn't feel like the right time.

So instead, I stand up and walk out of the room without bothering to wipe my face, leaving her lying on my bed, probably wondering what the fuck just happened. I don't look back as I leave and head downstairs, my cock growing soft as I descend into the kitchen area.

Aidan and Slade are sitting at the dining table with their laptops out. They both stop what they're doing and glance at me, Slade glaring as usual and Aidan with that same conflicted expression on his face.

Brick is nowhere to be seen, which leads me to believe he might have been watching from the hallway and headed off in the other direction when we were done. Just a feeling. The dirty perv is probably jerking off in his shower right now. Not that I can blame him. Not that I won't be doing the same thing later when I replay the film reel in my head.

"Wash your fucking face," growls Slade, eyeing the mess smeared across my mouth and chin. "You're a fucking disgrace."

I grin back at him. "You're just jealous. Want me to wipe some on you?"

He narrows his eyes at me. "She shouldn't be here. She's a distraction."

Aidan furrows his brow and runs his hand through his hair. "Yeah, Roman. You're reinforcing Slade's concerns right now. Don't make me regret my decision. Go clean yourself up, you dirty fuck."

"Jesus, I just had a bit of fun with her." I put my hands up in mock defense. "You heard her. I saved her life, and she wanted to thank me. That's all it was. You know that's how I operate. I love fucking women, and pussy means nothing to me. That's all she is, and I'd never let pussy get in the way of our business."

Everything I just said is usually factual. I don't attach feelings to women. They're just a means to an end, a way to achieve the pleasure that I'm constantly craving. It should be no different with Angel, and I didn't intend for it to be.

But as the words come out of my mouth, I realize I'm not so sure that's the case this time.

CHAPTER 30

ANGEL

My body is feeling pleasantly relaxed from multiple orgasms delivered by Roman's mouth and tongue, but my mind is a little confused by our encounter.

I was sure he was going to be selfish, to just stick his cock in me and make me reward him for saving my life by letting him fuck me, but it was quite the opposite.

He was all about pleasing me, worshipping me. I've never had my pussy eaten the way he feasted upon it, as if he was starving and the only thing he wanted to devour was me.

And then he didn't even try to fuck me. In some ways, I want to say I'm disappointed, because my body was and is still craving him inside me, definitely his cock or at least his fingers. But his tongue was so talented that it would be rude to say. I was most definitely satisfied without needing those things. He didn't even need to add anything beyond his tongue to make me orgasm multiple times.

While I still want to feel his cock buried deep inside me, I feel good, sated.

But my feelings of satiety are being overridden by invading

thoughts. Less pleasurable ones. There's too much on my mind. I'm worried about the guys inviting me to stay. It's a complex invitation and there's a lot to process.

They just murdered someone, and then someone tried to murder me and would have if the guys hadn't kidnapped me.

There are a lot of layers in this situation. A lot of volatility and uncontrollable variables.

If my crazy stalker hadn't gone and ransacked my salon and my apartment while attempting to find and slaughter me, what would these guys have done to me?

Because I strongly doubt they'd have said 'hey, just stay here and be our roommate because we've decided you're handy to have around.'

And what might they still do? I really don't know them all that well. It's only been a few days and the circumstances have hardly been normal.

I wonder if what happened between Roman and me, and before that Aidan and me, will change the dynamics in the house. What if the other guys don't like it, and want me gone? I'm pretty sure Slade already does. He's even told me as much. He already sees me as a threat. He hates me.

It's not like I have any other options other than trying my luck on the street. I don't think I'd last long out there, though, especially with *him* looking for me.

The thing is, I don't want to get my hopes up by staying here, thinking they really want me to be here for me. Because they could be doing this out of guilt, and from my experience, guilt wears off quickly.

They might change their mind and put me out on the street without any notice and then I'll be back to square one. Below square one, because at least I had a business and a home before, as modest as they may have been.

I can't go back to the salon and I can't go back to the apartment, that much is clear.

If I had to guess how comfortable they all are with the decision to invite me to stay, I think it's variable. I know for sure that Slade doesn't want me to be here. He's made that abundantly clear.

And it feels like Aidan is maybe on the fence, but for whatever reason is okay with it for right now.

Roman seems to want me around for sex... kind of, not that he'll actually fuck me, but who knows how long that will last?

And Brick is probably fine either way. He's a wildcard, and he doesn't seem to view life and death in the same way as anyone else I know.

I guess, for now, I'll stay and see what happens. It's the greatest shot I have at remaining alive at the moment, even though it's not guaranteed to last.

God knows Slade would off me in a second given the chance, and Brick is crazy enough that he just might help him.

Aidan might decide I'm too much of a risk to keep around.

For now, at least two, let's say two-point-five of them want me to stay.

But that means I'm going to have to let them help me, and I don't like that one bit.

Regardless of the quality of my accommodations, there's a killer on the loose. And he won't back off just because the thread count on my sheets has improved.

He's relentless, and he will stop at nothing until he gets what he wants.

Until he destroys me.

CHAPTER 31

ANGEL

The guys want to help take my mind off things, so we get up early and head out to one of their favorite breaks for a sunrise surf.

Even though it involves leaving the house for a bit, it feels like a safe option, and it's refreshing to be able to go outside.

There were no clues left at the salon that would tie me back to these guys. Roman was a walk-in, and The Asshole's body was long gone by the time Psycho McGee raided the place. Just a puddle of blood, and even though he's resourceful, there's no way he could have analyzed the guy's blood and tracked it back to us.

I know that sounds wacky, but he's incredibly resourceful and it's something he might try. At this point, I wouldn't put anything past him.

He's capable of anything, no matter how insane it sounds. Because he is fucking insane, the way no textbook could do justice.

There's no trace of the guys at my apartment, either. Brick's the only one who spent any time there prior to it being ransacked, and according to him, all he did was gather my stuff and shove it in a duffel bag. I have no doubt he rifled through my underwear drawer and sniffed my panties—and I know he kept at least one pair—but I doubt he would have left anything behind to link me to him.

Thankfully, this puts the lunatic on the back foot. He's tracked me to this island, but my apartment and salon are relatively far away from here. There's no logical connection between me and these guys, and no chance meeting or interaction online that he could stumble across. I haven't even had access to my phone since I've known them.

He's going to find me, and from how he's behaving I think it will be soon, but today I get to take a moment for myself.

A moment to back off from the coiled rubber band that feels like it's wrapped around my throat and my body at all times.

A moment to breathe.

The waves are mild, even though I know the guys could handle something way more intense. Growing up on the coastal mainland, the guys are used to volatile water, but they've decided to take me somewhere much calmer. And I need calm right now.

I have a feeling they brought me here so that I can join in and surf while they keep watch over me. Although I surf a few times a week, it's generally in gentle waves like this. There's a peace that comes with it, sitting atop these gentle rolling waves and letting you take them into shore. It's part of the reason I chose this island as my refuge.

They made it clear they didn't want me sitting on the beach by myself while they were out on the water. They didn't want me to be 'easy pickings', as Brick had put it, which sent a shiver up my spine as he said the words.

The thought of sitting on the sand, enjoying watching them surf, and suddenly being abducted by the lunatic, is the stuff of nightmares. I'm sure it will encroach on my dreams tonight or another night.

But, for now, I get to have a precious instant, a moment where I can forget the fear and darkness that I have learned I'll never escape.

Being around the ocean is therapeutic for me. When I'm in the water or coasting in on a wave, in those moments, I truly feel free. Like *he* can't get me. Like it's just me and the forces of nature propelling me.

I'm at the ocean's mercy, and it respects me as long as I respect it. If the ocean decided to take me under, it could, and I would be okay with it because it wouldn't be somebody else's decision.

Plus, it's something I get to enjoy alone, which is my preference for just about everything. The fewer people around you, the fewer people you let into your life, the less chance anybody will let you down.

It's different being out here with the guys than when I'm around my loose group of acquaintances, generally just paddling around by myself. I feel odd being part of a group activity where we're engaged in what everyone is doing, where I'm a member of this gang.

Lone wolves get all awkward when they're suddenly brought into a pack.

The guys show off a little while I'm out in the water with them. I dangle my legs over the side of my board a lot of the time, just sitting there and watching them having fun. But they also help to coach me and they clap and cheer loudly each time I catch a decent wave. Even when I wipe out spectacularly, they cheer me on to catch the next one.

The whole outing is fun and light. It frees my mind in the moments that demand my complete concentration, as well as the moments where I find my head empty, just floating on my board and hearing the water softly slap against it. It tests my body, my focus and my balance, and it also lets me relax in a way that I generally find very hard to do. It's just what I need.

When I get back to shore, I lift my board above me and rest it on top of my head, the way I prefer to carry it. My arms are too short to carry it underneath my armpit the way some people can.

As I walk inland, a voice calls out to me from the ocean and I turn around to look.

It's Aidan, also heading in, asking me to wait for them before I get too far away from the shoreline. I nod, the board bobbing above me, and turn back around toward the carpark area.

As I turn, the board making a wide rotation with me, I almost crash into someone heading in my direction. They're also carrying their board on top of their head, and the long slabs of fiberglass and epoxy almost smack into each other at above-head height. I reel back, dodging at the last moment, barely avoiding a collision. That wouldn't have been good.

"Watch it, bitch!" the other person hisses at me.

I take a closer look at them. It's another female, wearing bikini bottoms and a rash guard. She has cascading red hair with pink streaks, and she'd be very pretty if she wasn't narrowing her eyes and curling her lip at me in a snarl.

"Watch where the fuck you're going!" she growls, her eyes blazing.

I glare at her. "I turned around for one second because someone was calling out to me. You watch where the fuck you're going, *bitch*! Loving the female empowerment around here." I roll my eyes.

She glares at me and darts around my board and heads into the ocean, lowering her board into the water. My eyes follow her as she paddles, heading out to meet a group of guys waving at her from another nearby break.

I frown. Not because I can't handle a rude bitch, but because it's remotely unsettling when I feel like I do something wrong when it comes to surfing etiquette. It's intimidating, the surf culture, even though I'm also fascinated by it.

I don't know how I could have avoided that situation, and a flush creeps up my cheeks as I realize my guys, and maybe hers, all saw the interaction just now.

I probably look like an awkward idiot, almost crashing into someone more experienced than me with my board. They're probably all laughing at me out there. I feel frazzled, the buzz of my time in the water already starting to dissipate.

Again, I don't normally care what people think of me, but surfing gets me out of my comfort zone in the best and worst ways.

As I stand and worry about losing all credibility in the ocean, the four Brixtons emerge from the water. Aidan and Slade each carry their boards under an arm, and Brick and Roman carry theirs on top of their heads like me.

Both methods give me a nice view of their strong biceps and rippling abs, and the rising sun bathes each of them in a golden glow, as if they're gods and heaven is shining beams of light across their gorgeous bodies.

They're all magnificent. My pussy clenches as I think about the things I would do to all four of these men, and that I'd let them do to me. And the things that some of us have already done.

I'm kind of surprised that Roman would risk ruining his hair, resting the board on his head like that, but then I think back to how hard I pulled it on the bed while his tongue pierced my opening. Maybe he lets his hair standards slide when it comes to doing things he loves. Like surfing and feasting on pussy. Who knows?

"You okay?" asks Aidan, concern in his voice. "What happened back there?" He gestures towards the woman.

"Just a rude bitch," I shrug. "Nothing I can't handle."

"What did she say to you? It looked like you were arguing?"

"It's my fault, I guess. Turned around and almost smacked her board with mine. I'm mortified, honestly. But like I said, it's fine."

"Nah, I saw her coming straight for you at speed," says Slade. He rarely speaks, and he's never said a kind word toward me, so it's interesting he's decided to defend me now. "I wouldn't worry about anything she has to say, anyway."

"Wait, you know her? Who is she?" I'm suddenly curious. I know the island is small and everything, but this person has done enough for Slade to have an opinion that he's prepared to voice. Fascinating.

"She's with some guys we know," explains Aidan, running a hand through his hair. "Rivals, you might say. They're out there somewhere," he says, gesturing at the water behind him but not wasting effort to look in their direction.

"*With* them? Like in a gang?"

"Kind of," says Roman. "Although I believe she's also intimately acquainted with more than one of them, from what we've heard."

"They're like a bunch of Peter Pans," scoffs Slade. "They're all in their forties, but act like they just got out of high school, always joking around, even when things get serious. Calling each other bro this, bro that. Wearing tank tops and shorts like they're ten years old. There's something wacky about growing up on the island. All the sunshine and sea salt have got them thinking they're ageless. Peter fucking Pan losers."

I look out at the ocean and see her having what appears to be a fun time with the four guys she joined out at the break. They seem to be having a similar experience to us, the guys all showing off and having fun, her watching and joining in now and then.

One of them slowly surfs past her on a long, rolling wave, sits on his board and kisses her on his way by. She leans in, returning his kiss as he makes his way past.

"Well, what do you know? Good for her," I say. I can't help it. It just comes out.

She might be a rude bitch but she's doing something right if she's got four guys like that. I can't see them up close but I don't need to in order to know they're all hot and incredibly in shape.

"I didn't think something like that was possible. Truly good for her."

All four Brixtons glance at each other.

Brick wiggles his eyebrows.

Roman grins.

Aidan's expression is hard to pin down, but again I get the sense he's conflicted.

Slade scowls at me, his defense of me clearly only a passing reprieve.

I can't read their expressions, but it's like they're doing the silent communication thing again. God, they're frustrating. Grown men with their own secret non-verbal language, like they're psycho quadruplets.

"What?" I peer at them. "What's going on? Did I miss something?"

"Nothing," says Aidan, running a hand through his hair. He sighs. "Let's get back to the house. We have stuff to do. And we have something waiting for you at home."

———

As soon as we walk in the front door, my senses are assaulted by the overpowering fragrance of flowers. Walking into the kitchen, I see four enormous bouquets, each standing in an ornate vase, all in a row. They're artfully displayed, as if an actual florist spent hours tweaking every petal, every leaf, to the perfect angle to showcase the blooms.

"Oh my god. What are these? Is someone getting married?"

Aidan smirks. "These are to make you feel more comfortable, to make sure you know we want you to be here."

"Even you?" I narrow my eyes at Slade. "You got me one of these?"

"Don't push me," he growls, but his eyes are more gentle than usual.

"This is a lot of flowers," I say, walking closer to them. I lean in and sniff the first bouquet, and it smells heavenly. I close my eyes as I inhale the heady scent.

"We tried to get you one large one, but we couldn't agree on what best represented you," shrugs Roman. "We all have something we wanted to convey."

"Ha! I've barely received flowers from anyone, and when I did, I'm pretty sure they just grabbed the most basic offering from a nearby gas station. The whole nearly-dead roses in a plastic wrapping type of situation. Definitely not trying to convey anything except a desire to get into my pants. But this is... wow."

"Can you guess who got you which one?" grins Brick.

I look at the first bouquet and step closer to inspect it in more detail. It's colorful and elegant, a very full bouquet composed of a variety of flowers, including some bright yellow blooms that I recognize as carnations.

"Tell me more about the yellow carnations."

"Well, they're happy flowers, representing positive thinking. I thought they might help you get through this situation with the piece of shit that's stalking you."

"They also represent rejection, Roman," says Brick, his encyclopedic knowledge evidently extending from blood to floral symbolism.

"That seems accurate if these are from Roman," I say, with a hollow laugh. I swear, if that man doesn't let me sit on his cock soon, I'm going to explode.

"You called it, but not because of that," he huffs. "I had no idea they had that meaning. They just looked cheerful, and I wanted to make you smile given what you're going through."

"Sometimes it's the hidden meaning that means the most," I shrug, "but I'll take them at face value, I suppose. They're very pretty."

There's some fluffy greenery surrounding the blooms, which I recognize as fennel. "Is that in case I get hungry?" I grin at Roman.

"It's meant to represent flattery. I had to weave in my charming personality," he grins back, and I laugh. "Plus, it's not hard to flatter you. There are so many nice things to say." He grins at me.

I move to the second bouquet. It's quirky with a bunch of unique flowers I've never seen before, so I automatically assume it's from Brick.

"These are from you, I take it?" I ask, pointing at the bouquet.

Brick feigns surprise. "How did you know?"

"Maybe the skulls all over the vase gave it away, as well as whatever this sharp thing is sticking out the top looking like a torture implement," I laugh, and the others join me.

"They're not just any flowers, though," he says, proudly. "Want to know more about why I chose them?"

"Sure," I say, grinning. "Hit me."

"Well, obviously I have some black roses in there because they represent death and darkness, but they're also beautiful, like you. So that seemed appropriate, especially seeing you're my little Valkyrie. And then we have some chrysanthemums. They're meant to bring bad luck and nightmares."

"Gee, thanks," I say, and I can't help but laugh.

"No, you don't understand," says Brick, shaking his head. "My theory is, if you have these on your own terms, you get to control things. I know you have nightmares. Even when you're awake, sometimes, you'll go somewhere. I don't think you hear yourself scream, but I have. I want to put the control back in your hands."

"That's… quite sweet and thoughtful of you, Brick," I say cautiously.

He beams. "But wait, there's more! These ones," he says, pointing at an unusual flower with gray leaves and yellow petals that are almost sickly in tone but in a beautiful way, "are asphodels. They also symbolize death."

"Jesus, Brick. Should I be worried? Is this a death bouquet?"

"Death's coming for all of us, Angel," he says. "You may as

well embrace it, learn to soak it all in. I mainly got these because they look cool, but when you give them to someone, it's meant to mean your regrets will follow them into the grave. I figured they were fine because I don't have any regrets, so nothing will follow you in when you die."

"Jesus, Brick!" Slade can't hold his opinions in any longer.

"Fucking weirdo," Roman snorts at Brick, and I do the same.

"Then we have some bird's-foot trefoil," he says, pointing at some bright yellow blooms with flecks of orange. "These symbolize revenge and actually contain trace amounts of cyanide."

"Wow, you're really going for the death and revenge theme here," I laugh. "They're really pretty, though. I'll just make sure I don't accidentally steep them and turn them into tea."

"Would you expect anything less from me?" Brick grins and wiggles his eyebrows. I get the sense he had a lot of fun picking these out.

I move to the third bouquet. It's simple, with tiny and brilliant orange flowers that look like little clusters of flames. I've never seen these flowers before, but they're simple and captivating. Something about their depth and fury reminds me of Slade. "I'm guessing these are from you, but I don't know why I think that," I say, glancing at him.

I'm skeptical that he got me something so pretty, and that he didn't just wrap some garbage up in plastic and hand it to me instead.

He nods. "You got me."

"What are these flowers?" I ask, pointing to the flame-like clusters. "They're gorgeous."

"You might not think so when you know the meaning behind them," he says, smirking at me, his eyes developing a tinge of the cruel glimmer I've become accustomed to.

"Try me," I say, narrowing my eyes at him. Only Slade could buy me flowers to offend me. I'm ready for anything.

"They're butterfly weeds."

"Oh okay, got it. You got me weeds instead of flowers. That tracks," I say, rolling my eyes. "They're still gorgeous, so I don't care. Did you really think I'm that easily offended? Do you really think my sensibilities are so delicate?"

"Ha, you don't get it," Slade sneers. "They represent solitude and the rejection of others. When you give them to someone, you're essentially telling them you want them to *leave*. Get it? I want you to leave. To go away."

Even though it's coming from Slade, and therefore I should have expected it, his cruel words feel like a slap in the face. Everyone else has been so nice with this little exercise, but he's clearly determined to ruin it.

"Oh, and the other flowers in the bouquet?" he says. "They're orange lilies. They symbolize hatred and humiliation. I couldn't resist." He smirks at me, his eyes cold.

"Slade, knock it off, man," says Roman. "That was harsh."

My eyes flick to Roman. "You don't get to speak for me."

I turn back to Slade and narrow my eyes. "Fuck you, Slade," I say, my voice low and cold. I blink back tears and resist the urge to run from the room. Or at least to grab the vase and dump them in the kitchen's large trash can. He clearly got these to upset me and delighted in telling me why he chose them. I can't give him the satisfaction of knowing he won. "I'm disappointed, Slade. No black dahlias? I don't know much about flowers, but I know they represent evil and dishonesty and betrayal. I think they would have been much more appropriate coming from you. Maybe some tansies to visually represent your uncalled-for hostility against me."

Brick lets out a low whistle as if to diffuse the palpable tension in the kitchen.

Sticking my jaw out so it doesn't tremble, not waiting for a response from Slade, I move to the fourth bouquet. "Anyway," I say, sniffing. "This one must be from you, Aidan." He smiles as I glance in his direction.

It's a simple bouquet, neatly organized with only a few

different flower varieties. If it wasn't the last bouquet, I still would have guessed it was from him by the way it's been methodically arranged without any extra fluff.

Like Brick, he also selected some black roses.

"To symbolize revenge, because we're going to help you exact yours on your stalker," he explains. "They're a reminder that we're here for you. We're going to protect you, Angel. We will never let anything bad happen to you as long as you're with us. And you can ignore Slade," he narrows his eyes at him, "because he doesn't represent our collective view."

We return our attention to the fourth bouquet.

"What are these?" I ask, pointing at some pretty purple flowers.

"They're clematis," nods Aidan. "They're the 'queen of the vines' and represent…" He pauses and a flush creeps across his cheeks as if he's embarrassed by what he's about to share. "They represent mental beauty. They reminded me of you."

"Oh my gosh, Aidan, that's really sweet," I say, a flush building on my face, and I can't resist getting on my tiptoes and kissing him on his cheek.

"And then there's some dill because it's meant to be powerful against evil. And some gardenia, because you're meant to give them to someone who you think is lovely."

I smile at him. Of course, he'd thought this bouquet through as carefully as he does everything else.

"Thanks so much, all of you. All of you except Slade." I narrow my eyes and glare at him. "When I met you, I never thought the five of us would be standing here while three of you share how thoughtfully you picked these out for me. I feel so spoiled," I say, smiling at them.

"Actually, I take that back. All four of you. Even you, Slade. I'm going to channel the hatred in your selections. Take it as a sign that you spend far too much time thinking about me. Even though your bouquet was very cruel, clearly you must have put a lot of thought into it."

He grimaces, eyes narrowed at me. I appear to have hit a nerve.

After dealing with my psycho stalker for years, there's one thing I'm clear on.

Whether thoughts are loving or dark, they're still thoughts, obsessions, and energy focused on someone. That energy, whether it starts from dark or light, can be transformed and channeled and used in the ways you want.

You can make of Slade's thoughts what you will, but his mind is definitely on me, whether he likes it or not. And I intend to use his energy for my benefit.

CHAPTER 32

AIDAN

"Hey," says Roman loudly, drawing all of our eyes to him. "Did you guys notice that a bunch of the options reminded you of those assholes that claim to protect the island?"

"Sounds like you have a crush," snorts Brick. "Did you want to get them a bouquet, too?"

Angel snorts.

"Actually, I did," Roman shrugs.

"What the fuck, man?" Slade winces at Roman. "Are you going to take them to a dinner and a movie next, and maybe buy them a box of chocolates so they'll suck your dick?"

"No, what I sent was just fine. If they know anything about flowers, the meaning will be loud and clear. It was too perfect to resist."

"What did you send them? Not poison ivy?" I ask, raising an eyebrow.

"That would be too literal," shrugs Roman. "I sent them a bouquet of aster."

"What the hell is that?" asks Slade.

"It's this purple flower, kind of matches Angel's hair," he says, glancing at Angel. "It's meant to ward off snakes, keep them away. I was sending them a message."

"Yeah, a message you want to jump their bones, you fucking idiot," sneers Slade. The rest of us laugh.

"Hey, it made sense at the time," says Roman, crossing his arms tightly over his chest. "I wanted to send them aconite because it represents hatred and would have made their skin itch and burn, but for some reason, the florist didn't carry it."

I can't tell for sure, but it looks like Roman might be flushing slightly under his tan.

This is what happens when I don't micromanage these guys. And why I always have my eye on the weird shit they come up with independently.

"What? I sent them a warning. The asters say exactly what I meant them to," says Roman defensively.

"I don't think it's the type of flower you sent them that's the issue, Roman," I say, exasperated. "It's the fact you sent our enemies a bouquet of pretty flowers and they're going to be wondering what the fuck your intentions are." I shake my head and the others laugh.

Angel seems to be particularly amused by this development, her neck tilting back to expose her throat as she cracks up at Roman's expense.

We haven't figured out what we're going to do with her yet. And we haven't dealt with the very real threat against her. But just for this moment, for this snapshot in time, she looks happy, lighter, as if her problems are far away and she's just in the moment.

I'm glad that Roman sent flowers to our enemies, even if they think he's trying to date them all. Because it made Angel laugh, and right now her happiness is the only thing I care about.

CHAPTER 33

ANGEL

For a moment, for one precious and irreplaceable instant, I feel joy. These four guys went out of their way for me, to distract me and just give me a second to breathe.

They cared enough to plan out a surfing trip, to have bouquets deposited in the house while we were out. They'd each chosen them so carefully, even Slade, who channeled all his hatred for me into the tiny little blooms that look like flames.

It was a relief, a release to be able to laugh and howl at Roman's accidental romantic undertones toward the snakes. If only I could be a fly on the wall when the flowers arrive and they see his note. *'Standing in the flower shop, when I saw these, all I could think about was you guys.'* That's what he told us he sent them. I almost became deceased when he shared that part of the story, I was laughing so hard.

Now that the flower shenanigans are over, we've moved into the living room. Despite the tight squeeze, all four guys are on the couch with me like none of them could stand to be further away, even Slade. I'm sandwiched between Brick and Roman's large thighs and each has a hand protectively on my legs.

As Brick casually flicks through channels, finding something to watch, I stop him as an image I recognize appears on the screen.

"Wait, Brick, go back." I grab his arm. "Two channels back, I think it was."

He scrolls back twice and the screen lights up with what looks like an infomercial. Emblazoned in a banner across the bottom of the screen is 'Angel's Hair Salon'. My logo, just the way I designed it. But I've never taken out an ad, let alone a TV infomercial. I bet this cost a fortune. An uneasy feeling plants itself in the pit of my stomach and little goosebumps emerge on my arms.

"Turn it up," I direct Brick, and he adjusts the volume as a jingle begins.

"Get your sharpening on
At Angel's Salon
Do-do-do-do-do
You'll look your best
We'll peel your flesh
And stab you with a knife
We'll slit your throat from ear to ear
Your head will fall forward in the chair
You're living your best life!
I was a slutty whore back home
And nothing much has changed
But now I'm living on an island
Acting quite deranged
At Angel's… at Angel's…. Saloooooooooooon."

The screen fades to black.

"What the hell did we just watch?" asks Slade. "Because, uh, that marketing is something…" His voice trails off.

"I take it that's not something you created," says Aidan.

"Jesus," says Brick, turning off the TV.

"He's a real sicko, isn't he?" says Roman. "Fucking hell. How did that get past the censors?"

"I know, right? I thought I was in a dream because it was so off the wall. My logo, a shot of my salon before it was destroyed. But you're all apparently experiencing it, too."

"Can multiple people hallucinate together?" asks Brick. "I've always wondered about group hallucinations."

"He has basically unlimited resources. I'm sure it will get yanked at some point when people complain, but for now… it's live."

"He paid money for that. It was really weird," says Slade. "Clearly sending you a message. Fucking with you. I just don't know how he knew for sure you'd be watching."

"I don't know that it would matter if she did or not," says Aidan, running his hand through his hair. "He could have narrowed down the algorithm, targeted her demographics for the primary audience, but our TV is linked to our preferences, not hers. In my view, it doesn't matter if she was one of the first to watch it or not. This ad is insane, and it's going to blow up on social media in no time. He's going to make sure her business dies and has no chance of ever being revived. This is a sick smear campaign."

"He's going to destroy the one thing I built before he kills me," I say softly. "This will never be over. Until the day he kills me."

I want to say more, but that's all I'm able to say before there's a large bang and the compound is plunged into darkness.

***

Ready to keep reading? Here's a sneak peek of Book #2 in the Blood & Sand Series, *Sea of Snakes:*

Devon

The flight attendant peers at me from the aisle, her mouth moving while my music plays at full blast. She smiles at me, but it's forced politeness. Her flat eyes defy her by communicating something more like she wishes everyone on this plane would fuck off and die.

It must be a tough job some days, trapped in a sky pencil with a bunch of demanding assholes. I can't really blame her.

I remove my headphones and sit up in my chair. "Sorry, what?"

"Would you like a beverage?" she asks, enunciating each syllable, her gaze and body language clearly trying to convey she wants me to hurry and either order or not. I don't know how many times she probably has to repeat the same questions over and over, constantly drowned out by earbuds and headphones and the dull hum of the plane's engine.

"Just a Diet Coke," I reply.

She nods and then cracks open a can on her cart. She scoops some ice into a plastic cup and hands both the can and the ice-filled cup to me. "Here you go."

"Thank you." I smile back, mirroring her fuck-you gaze with my own, and roll my eyes as soon as she attends to another passenger. I only ordered a soda so I could get the plastic cup.

As soon as she moves beyond our row, I reach down and pull three flight bottles of Jack out of my carry-on bag and open them one by one, placing them on my fold-out tray.

My father hears the *click-click* sound of the opening of the bottles, and it rouses him from his nap. "Devon, you're not meant to do that, you know. It's against flight regulations."

I give him a sideways glance and slowly pour all three bottles into my cup without breaking eye contact. I raise the cup to my lips and take a long sip, enjoying the taste as the amber liquid streams down my throat, creating a pleasant and familiar burning sensation.

"Since when have you ever given a shit about following the

rules, Frank?" He lost the honor of being called Dad a long time ago. "Seems a bit late to start now, don't you think?"

He snorts because he knows I have a point.

My father and I have a strange, strained relationship. He's not a good person, and god knows, neither am I, but I've decided for various reasons to keep him in my life rather than estranging him. As an adult, we're past the point where I feel he can hurt me much anymore. Plus, we made an agreement a while ago that I'd go on a 'family' vacation with him once per year.

My trust fund is riding on that little requirement. Yes, I have a trust fund. Judge me. I couldn't care less. But I don't have access to most of it yet. Maybe I never will, because he keeps changing the rules surrounding it. Hell, knowing him, maybe it doesn't even exist anymore. I wouldn't put it past him to have spent it all already.

I'm not positive about why he keeps stringing me along like this. Sometimes I think it makes him feel like a better person having his daughter in his life. Or maybe he just likes to exert control over me because he can. He certainly did when I was a child, and maybe he just wants to carry it on into my adulthood the only way he knows how. I've thought about telling him to go fuck himself many times, and I might do that one day, but for now, we're stuck with each other for one week every year.

That's why I'm here, on a plane with my father, flying to a tropical island. While I like the ocean, these types of colorful, kitschy tourist destinations are totally not my vibe—it's hard to pull me out of the grungy stickiness of a city that's jam-packed with dive bars and a good music scene—but I let him pick the destination this time. He was strangely insistent on this specific location, which is weird because previously he's let me choose. He said he had some business to do here.

I'll worry about that later, though. Right now, I just want to make it through this plane flight and get to the hotel. Maybe I'll even find some excitement on this vacation

I take another long, satisfying sip of my whiskey, and wipe my mouth with the back of my hand. Sinking back into my chair, I replace my headphones and close my eyes.

***

Skyler

"You teaching a lesson today?" Zeke glances at me from the other side of the living room as he pulls a tank top over his head, grazing it past his closely cropped dark hair.

I don't think I've ever seen him wearing anything on his top half other than a tank top. I can hardly talk, but I manage to pull on an actual T-shirt from time to time, occasionally even a polo.

He has no interest in dressing to impress anyone, though, ever. His imposing, muscular body and tall frame do that on their own. The way he's built, he could probably walk around naked and get anything he wanted. Which I've actually seen him do a few times, now that I think about it.

"Yeah, a bit later on," I nod. "You guys want to meet me over at the break?"

The surf forecast is looking decent today. Nothing too wild, but it should be fun catching a few long ones into shore. It's always fun showing off in front of the tourists who are just learning, and who can barely get on a board, let alone ride a wave. Show them who's boss, who owns the place. Maybe snag a phone number or two. Living on an island has its advantages.

"Yeah, I'm planning to head out that way. Have some stuff to pick up for our next job. I'll see you out there." It's hard to keep Zeke out of the water, so I'm not surprised he's game to meet up. When he manages to pull himself away from work, that is. Surfing and work, Zeke's two vices.

"What about you, Dom?" I glance over at the burly guy who's sitting on an armchair that looks almost comically small for his expansive frame.

"Nah, man." He gestures at his muscular chest. "I'm going to get a tattoo, remember?" He had mentioned that, but I'd forgotten. There's been so much going on lately that it's been hard to keep track. "The snake on a surfboard."

"Oh, sweet," I nod. "Then we'll all have them finally, although I'm surprised you found a spare space to put it. But I'm glad you're getting it. The mark that shows everyone who we are, and what they can expect when we're in the ocean."

"Fuck yeah! I'm stoked about this one." He grins.

"Two to four weeks off surfing though, bro, while your skin heals. I don't know how you'll manage that." I can't remember a day that Dom hasn't been in the ocean since I've known him, let alone two full weeks away from it. He'd go insane. The sea is part of him. It runs through his veins, almost as much as it does mine and Zeke's. Dom's technically a transplant from the mainland, unlike us, but you'd never know it to look at him or to see him surf.

"Fuck waiting for it to heal," he says with a scoff, curling his upper lip. "The salt will help it heal faster. Plus, I'm not that soft. You really think I follow doctor's instructions for shit like that?"

"Yeah, I guess not." I shrug. He has a point. Dom's not one for rules. None of us are. And he certainly isn't a stranger to pain and suffering. In fact, I'm pretty sure he's been through so much that he's grown to like it.

Zeke narrows his eyes and snaps. "Stop chit-chatting, anyway, you lazy fucks." He's clearly over this back-and-forth which ironically he started, and is ready to get back to work.

He's a very intense person, and it's something I both admire and detest about him. As a somewhat serious person myself, even I sometimes wish he'd lighten up. I don't give myself a lot of downtime, because there's money to be made and an island to protect, but Zeke takes things to the next level.

"What time did you get done last night?" He glances over at Rake, who's laying back on the tattered couch with his cap pulled over his eyes. He doesn't respond as he's dozed off, and Zeke walks over to him, rips his cap from his head and throws it across the room. "Answer me, you fucking slacker!"

Rake, startled, snaps to attention and rears his fist back, instinctively readying to punch whoever has woken him from his slumber.

"Knock it off, both of you," I call out.

"Why? You're worried you're going to get hurt?" scoffs Zeke. He's clearly woken up on the wrong side of the bed this morning. Or, knowing him, he didn't get any sleep at all. He probably worked through the night.

"I could easily take both of you." I'm a good fighter, but so are they, and I don't need to show any sign of weakness, even around them. They may be like brothers to me, but sometimes I struggle to trust them, even though I trust them more than I do myself. They've never let me down so far. Whereas I've let myself down plenty of times. "We've got shit to do, and can't risk another visit to the hospital before we go sort those assholes out. They were trying to cut in on us again and I'm sick of them pulling that shit. They're always trying to cut in on our business and our waves, and they're little piss ants who don't stand a chance, but they keep trying anyway."

"What's happening again?" Rake rubs his eyes as they take their time to adjust to the light after his nap.

"Oh, for fuck's sake, man. Do we have to tell you everything three times? I need you to be more on top of things." Zeke sneers at Rake, who rolls his eyes in response.

"Stop antagonizing each other or I'll have Dom beat the crap out of both of you," I snarl at them, while Dom cracks his scarred knuckles and grins.

It's not unusual for Rake to carry on like this, bickering like an idiot, but it's less common for Zeke. It feels unnatural to take on a pseudo-parental role with them, breaking up their juvenile arguments. They're my age, after all. But Zeke and I both regularly seem to find ourselves in that position even though Zeke has found himself right in the middle of this particular situation. Being on the islands in a sheltered environment hasn't forced any of us to grow up, I guess you might say. I've heard it referred to as Peter Pan syndrome, and watching the way Rake and—hell, all of us—behave, it's a real thing.

Something's up with Zeke today, though. I can feel it. He's hypercritical and seems ready to lash out at the smallest thing. It's definitely not the first time Rake's had a power nap. He lives for power naps. Zeke knows this, and it's usually not a big deal.

"Mind telling us why you're so agitated today, Zeke? More than usual, I mean?"

His frown grows deeper. "The Brixtons, those slimy fuckers."

He spits out the name of our major rivals as his lips curl with rage. It's not too hard to get Zeke worked up about certain things, the Brixtons being one of them, but his fuse is ultra-short today.

"They really have been trying to cut in on our business. They intercepted our last haul, and I think they're trying to take our place here. I know you don't think much of them, but I'm concerned we've been underestimating their strength and how far they're prepared to go to take over from us. They're not as weak as you seem to think they are, and they've been taking some big swings at our territory recently."

"How do you know it was them?" I raise an eyebrow. The last haul was in transit only a few hours ago, and it seems like a quick turnaround to find out both what happened and who did it.

"One of their guys got sloppy down at the dive bar after a few too many shots," Zeke shrugs. "They told a few people, and word got straight back to me. They were downright giddy about it, apparently. Think they're the top dogs now."

I guess that's the advantage of having a dive bar on the island that opens at six in the morning. Some people just can't help themselves from heading down there first thing and over-sharing their life stories and other secrets. It also helps that we have some trusted contacts who spend a lot of time there gathering intel. Loose lips sink ships.

"Fuck that!" Rake, now fully awakened from his nap, stands

up and clenches his tattooed fists at his sides. "Nobody takes our shit! Nobody fucks with us. We're the top dogs around here. I'm going over there right now."

He charges toward the door, but I reach up and grab him by the back of his tank top and pull him back into the living room.

"Easy now, Rake," I warn. "I don't doubt you could take them by yourself, but let's be strategic about this."

Rake's a skilled fighter and his height has definite advantages, but sometimes his judgement isn't the best. There's no need for him to charge into a fight solo against ten or more guys who are likely armed and just as good at fighting as he is.

"Yeah, and I'm getting my tattoo done today," adds Dom, glancing at his chest again, apparently prioritizing his body art above our business interests. "I've put down a huge deposit and have already had to reschedule twice. They said they'll just keep the money if I can't come in today."

"Glad you're putting our business first, bro." Zeke glares at Dom, his rage at the Brixton brothers diverting to him. "Do we need to teach you about priorities? Because I'll fucking show you, boy!"

"You'll show me, *boy*? You sound just like your dad, talking like that." Dom's eyes glimmer cruelly at Zeke, who flinches almost imperceptibly. This conversation is going completely off the rails. The comment clearly stung. It's a low blow, and not entirely inaccurate.

"Gotta give me more credit than that. I'm not a completely evil piece of shit." Zeke runs his fingers through his hair and looks at the ground, his voice low. None of us has a father to be proud of.

"Hang on, both of you." I put my hand out in what I hope is a peaceful gesture. I need to de-escalate this situation, and we don't have time for this unproductive back-and-forth.

"Listen for a sec. I agree that Dom's priorities are off and he needs to sort himself out and soon. But, there's a benefit to thinking this through more carefully. Rather than rushing in there half-assed. Otherwise, we risk making a fool of ourselves in front of those shitheads, and compromising our credibility with Tane."

"Well, I disagree," says Rake. He crosses his arms tightly over his chest, revealing ropy, well-developed muscles often overshadowed by his tall figure. "But I'll go along with it this time so Dom can try to turn himself into a pretty boy and make his body look better for the ladies."

Dom narrows his eyes and spits in Rake's direction, and Rake only just dodges the saliva flying out of the other man's mouth.

"Fuck, you're a bunch of mongrels," says Zeke.

"Yeah, like you aren't," snarls Rake.

Both of them are right. And these days, everyone's been on a knife edge.

***

Devon

After arriving at the hotel and checking in, I put my bag in my room, and don't even stop to check out the space.

Instead, I apply a dollop of sunscreen to my face and shoulders and arms, inspect the map of the hotel provided by the front guest agent and make my way to the bar. That's where I gravitate when I visit most places, but especially when I have to go on vacation with my father. Somewhere with stiff drinks, where I can drown out other people and their bullshit, and dull all the terrible memories.

While I'm not here for the architecture, I can't help but notice the grandeur of the space as I move through the foyer, following the map's directions.

The high ceilings make room for elaborate chandeliers, and giant art pieces adorn the walls in the open-air space. Lively island music pipes in from invisible speakers, and the area abuzz with people dressed in tropical attire. Conversations ebb and flow as people discuss their vacation plans with palpable excitement. Discreet air fresheners shoot out some kind of floral fragrance—hibiscus maybe—and it intertwines with the briny scent of the nearby ocean.

Down an expansive hallway, I see an oceanfront event lawn, where a crowd of hotel staff scurry around setting up banquet tables in front of a stage. Decadent bouquets cascade across table runners, and candles adorn each table setting. I'm not sure, but it could be a luau or a wedding. I keep walking and make a left into another area filled with overpriced high-end hotel stores, and then a right which takes me outside toward the beach.

The humid air hits me as I walk outside and leave the comfort of the air conditioning behind. The intense sun beats down from a cloudless sky. Even though I applied sunscreen, I know if I don't stay out of the sun, I'll quickly turn into a lobster or all of my freckles will connect.

After navigating the maze-like path, I find the hotel bar right where the map said it should be. It's an open-air structure with seats surrounding it in a horseshoe shape covered by a thatched roof. Hungry seagulls and other birds roam the area looking for crumbs. Occasionally, when someone's not looking, one will jump right up and steal a truffle fry or a piece of poke. While I could sit at one of the standalone high-tops or a regular table, I always feel more comfortable sitting at the bar than being served by someone at a table. Being right beside the bar also usually means I can get my drinks more quickly.

Unfortunately for me, this bar is one of those spots that makes frilly tropical drinks. Things like mai tais with elaborate pineapple and cherry garnishes, which are at least boozy, and frozen monstrosities like Miami Vices and Piña Coladas. Gross. There's no way I'm ordering one of those garish things.

Instead, I order my signature shot of whiskey, and then on second thought I ask the bartender to make it two. He raises an eyebrow, not seeing a companion with me. I guess it's not a common request at a place like this, but then he sees I'm serious and pours me two shots, neat as requested. I chug back both and ask for a third. He shrugs and half-grins as he grabs the bottle to refill one of my glasses. "Getting your vacation started off the right way?"

"Something like that." I smile and shrug. He's accurate. I need to get into vacation mode. I can barely tolerate my father when I'm sober, so I need to loosen up a little.

While I'm sitting here, I get a message on my phone and see it's from my friend Donkey, checking in to see if I've survived the flight with my dad. We call him that because he once sent a dick pic to his mom by mistake, and it's just kind of stuck. It's a silly name for a pretty serious guy. I send him back a picture of my whiskey shot and he responds with a cheers and thumbs-up emoji.

He's one of my friends who also comes from a broken place and has endured so much pain in his life. We don't have a ton of superficial stuff in common, and it's like we've gravitated together because of the darkness we've each endured. While our specific experiences have been different, they've changed both of us forever, and we recognize that in each other.

I've learned that darkness attracts darkness, and some might think it's sad, but I think it's quite beautiful. He's one of the few friends that I've let into my world, that knows some of what I've been through, and even then I wouldn't say we're *super* close. But he's really all I've got.

***

Skyler

On my way to the beach for a quick surf, before I teach a lesson, I decide to cut through the bar. We're not meant to do that—me in particular—but it's quicker and I don't care too much about rules. Besides, I'm not planning on sticking around.

Tony, the bartender on duty, nods at me. "Hey, Sky!" He calls out, waving as I get closer. He knows I'm not supposed to be here, but he doesn't care. I nod back and grin, pointing at the ocean, and he nods again.

As I walk past the bar area, I see someone who doesn't look quite like they belong. And that's a good thing because I don't think much of most of the people that typically come here. The girl hunches over her phone with her hand cupped around a shot of what appears to be whiskey. Something you don't see people drinking much of around here.

At a glance, I can see she's not like all the other guests, each trying to outdo the next with their high-end fashion. The typical patrons wear their diamonds down to the bar and order cliché drinks to take photos of for Instagram. Then they complain when their priceless jewels get lost in the sand or the sea. The folks with metal detectors can make some really good money from what they find on the strip of beach in front of this and the other neighboring luxury hotels.

This stranger, however, is fucking stunning and is definitely not covered in diamonds. She's wearing all black and gray, a fitted tank top and shorts. Her look is a stark contrast compared to all the bright, tropical prints people wear on their island vacations. Not what I'm used to seeing around here at all. Tony notices me looking at her and he winks at me from the bar, a cheeky grin on his face. I guess she stood out to him, too.

The other patrons are engaging in shallow chit-chat, probably about their hometowns and how they would never want to live on the island full-time. Boring jerks. It's actually disgusting hearing how they trash our home casually, bar side, when they think nobody local is listening. But she doesn't look like she's interested in interacting with anyone or anything other than her shot of whiskey and whatever's on the other end of her phone.

Just by looking at her, I get the vibe that she does what she wants without giving a shit about what anybody else thinks. She's clearly not trying to fit in at this bar, anyway.

She's fixated on her phone and doesn't look up, but I can tell by her profile that she's drop-dead gorgeous. She has high cheekbones and full, red lips. Smoky liner and long, dark eyelashes frame her eyes. Her red hair cascades down her back like waves of fire, and it's highlighted with streaks of pale pink that should look unnatural yet look perfect on her. Leaning over her phone, she shows off a hint of her cleavage. As I walk past her, my cock twitches.

I see a lot of pretty women at the beach, toned and tanned in their bikinis. I'm a good-looking guy and I'm confident. With a constant coming and going of tourists with loosened inhibitions on their vacations, I have access to all the pussy I want. So I'm kind of surprised by the effect this woman is having on me. There's something about her that's captivating me at a glance. I'm not used to it, and it's an interesting new feeling.

I don't stop to approach her, though, because even though I have great flirting game, I'm almost late for work and my chosen brothers and I have caused trouble at this bar one too many times. Hotel management has instructed us not to come back, at least for a while, and I don't want to press my luck.

It's okay, though. She stands out so much that I'm confident I'll be able to track her down later…

He didn't follow her.
He memorized her.

KEEP READING NOW.
SEA OF SNAKES (Blood & Sand #2) is available here: https://amzn.to/41W8LHa
Devon didn't come here to belong to anyone…
but the island doesn't let things go.

Want bonus scenes + early release alerts?
Join my reader list here:

https://heidistark.myflodesk.com/gglvf1vaw3
No spam. Just chaos.

Blood & Sand Series (Dark Why Choose Romance)
- Sea of Sinners (Book 1)
- Sea of Snakes (Book 2)

These books must be read in order:
- Sea of Rage (Book 3)
- Sea of Pain (Book 4)
- Sea of Demons (Book 5)
- Sea of Redemption (Book 6)

Want something darker than dark romance?

If you like psychological survival stories about obsession, control, and emotional destruction, start my pitch-black thriller duet:
- Pretty Red Flags (Book 1)
- Beautiful Terror (Book 2)

In the mood for a spicy palate cleanser?

Check out my why choose rugby romcom:
- Quick Tap
- Rucked

Join me on social media:

Facebook: @heidistarkauthor
Instagram: @heidistarkauthor
TikTok: @heidistark_author
Bluesky: @heidistarkauthor
Website: https://heidistarkauthor.com

WANT MORE THAN WHAT'S ON THE PAGE?

Then come a little closer, my darling.

Hang out in my Reader Group – Where we obsess over morally gray men, spiral over cliffhangers, and indulge in the kind of bookish chaos that doesn't stay contained to the story.

Get my Newsletter – Early access. Exclusive scenes. Teasers you won't see anywhere else.

You like knowing what happens next… don't you?

I share early access to my books, bonus scenes, and exclusive content with a select group of readers who don't mind things getting a little dark.

If that's you, apply here.

Just don't say I didn't warn you.

Welcome to my world.
You're not getting out of it.

ABOUT HEIDI STARK

Heidi Stark writes contemporary dark romance with a twist of danger, desire, and the occasional sports scandal.

Known for her badass heroines and irresistibly morally grey men, Heidi has captivated readers with 20+ titles, including the gripping *Blood and Sand* series, the fiery *Volcano of Pain*, and her highly anticipated new release, *Beautiful Terror*.

Originally hailing from the lush landscapes of New Zealand, Heidi now calls the U.S. home, where she shares her creative chaos with her feline sidekick, Fang.

When she's not crafting heart-pounding stories, Heidi is a whirlwind of energy—hitting up barre classes, devouring true crime podcasts, dabbling in roller derby, people-watching, or indulging in her guilty pleasure: reality TV binges. Always on the hunt for inspiration, she's probably plotting her next book—or her next travel adventure

Dark, daring, and deliciously addictive—Heidi's world is one you'll never want to leave.

Join Heidi on socials!

- Tiktok: @heidistark_author
- Facebook: @heidistarkauthor
- Instagram: @heidistarkauthor
- Threads: @heidistarkauthor
- Bluesky: @heidistarkauthor
- Rednote: @heidistarkauthor
- Goodreads
- Bookbub
- Amazon
- Website: https://heidistarkauthor.com